THE EXQUISITE

THE EXQUISITE

A NOVEL

LAIRD HUNT

COFFEE HOUSE PRESS
MINNEAPOLIS
2006

COPYRIGHT © 2006 by Laird Hunt
COVER AND BOOK DESIGN by Linda Koutsky
AUTHOR PHOTOGRAPH © Lorna Hunt

COFFEE HOUSE PRESS books are available to the trade through our primary distributor, Consortium Book Sales & Distribution, 1045 Westgate Drive, Saint Paul, MN 55114. For personal orders, catalogs, or other information, write to: Coffee House Press, 27 North Fourth Street, Suite 400, Minneapolis, MN 55401.

Coffee House Press is a nonprofit literary publishing house. Support from private foundations, corporate giving programs, government programs, and generous individuals helps make the publication of our books possible. We gratefully acknowledge their support in detail in the back of this book.

To you and our many readers around the world, we send our thanks for your continuing support.

FROM THE AUTHOR:
Special thanks for help in shaping *The Exquisite* go out to my fabulous editor, Chris Fischbach (a.k.a. Fish), and to my fabulous partner in literary and extra-literary adventures, Eleni Sikelianos.

LIBRARY OF CONGRESS CIP INFORMATION
Hunt, Laird.
The exquisite / Laird Hunt.
p. cm.
ISBN-13: 978-1-56689-187-5 (alk. paper)
ISBN-10: 1-56689-187-6 (alk. paper)
I. Title.
PS3608.U58E97 2006
813'.6—dc22
2006011901

FIRST EDITION | FIRST PRINTING
1   3   5   7   9   10   8   6   4   2
PRINTED IN CANADA

Ficnon
H9416e
10.06

for Eva Grace

I fainted during a bit of my life. I regained consciousness without any memory of what I was, and the memory of who I was suffers for having been interrupted. There is in me a confused notion of an unknown interval, a futile effort on the part of my memory to want to find that other memory. I don't connect myself with myself. If I've lived, I forget having known it.

> Fernando Pessoa
> The Book of Disquiet

I entered. I shut the door. I sat down on the bed. The blackest space spread out before me.

> Maurice Blanchot
> Death Sentence

ONE

Uh, uh, no way, I don't want it. But you *will* have it, Henry, you *must* have it, my dear friend Mr. Kindt once told me. My dear friend who is now dead.

You most certainly were. Indeed you did. Is that so, my dear boy? That's the way he talked. He would hold his hands up to the light and say, aren't they marvelous? He seemed to be particularly in love with his left arm. A rough patch of skin could send him into a sulk. His favorite word was *alluvial*. All the worn beauty of our weary old world in that word, he would say. In his apartment this was. One of those once-handsome buildings, turn of the last century, formerly elegant, now covered in dark netting, bricks crumbling, bludgeoned by time. We would sit there in his living room and eat meat or fish with heavy sauce and drink brandy, and he would talk. My God he would talk, his hands moving like strange moths above the meat.

The first time I saw Mr. Kindt I was standing in the middle of his living room holding a flashlight. Go there, he has things, my friend Tulip had told me. He did have things. Glass beakers and microscopes and anatomical charts and globes and maps and aluminum newspaper weights and a framed poster of a Rembrandt painting of a dissection.

Salamanders and small animals and small other things, some possibly alive, but most definitely dead, in jars. And things moving. Things rustling. Things moaning and things howling. And the whole place cold and filled with mist or smoke. I was just standing there taking it in, thinking, yeah, there are some things here, then someone said, hello, Henry.

Who is that? I said.

My name is Aris Kindt, I am the curator of this odditorium, the voice said.

I took a deep breath, tried to see through the mist, the stuff, the smells and sounds.

I saw you leave, I said. You went down the stairs, you got into a cab.

Are you sure I did? Are you sure it was *me*? This is, after all, in at least one of its guises, a city of subtle simulacra, of deceptive surfaces, of glib and phantom shimmerings.

How do you know my name?

There was a laugh: a box full of electric lightbulbs being stepped on, a school of small frozen fists shattered against a wall. The voice said, shine your torch over here.

"Over here" was onto the back of an enormous leather chair.

I watched you leave and I watched you get into a taxi and I came straight up here, I said.

Perhaps then, Henry, there is more than one of me, said the voice.

I didn't say anything. I could hear my heart beating in my ears. Sweat was starting up along the inside of my thighs.

He laughed again. Don't just stand there, do come around.

I went around. Mr. Kindt, the guy I had seen get into a cab, a cab that had driven off, was sitting there, quite naked. There were wires taped to his chest, and he was holding a monitor in his lap, and for a time the two of us held our positions and watched the steady green light make its way across the dark of the screen, and he looked up at me and said, do you see? and although the sweat had spread to my shoulders and temples and my heart was now as loud as a nail driver, I said, yes, and he said, aren't I lovely?

My friend's name was Tulip, and through her I met a man named Aris Kindt, who used to invite me over to his apartment and serve me plates of meat or fish, and in this way, and in others, I came to think of him as my dear friend. Herring was both served and the subject of conversation during our meeting. Herring, he would say, is holy. Herring, Henry, is God come to us as a fish. Herring is what was meant in the Gospels. Herring is the divine intricacy. Herring grows luminous when it dies, as, it has been said, did the corporeal Christ when he died, or numinous God, when he will die, or did die, and it tastes smashing, hot or cold. Pickled was mostly how Mr. Kindt liked his herring. In a creamy sauce. He would say, here is how you eat it, and he would eat it, and then I would eat it, and at first I could not quite believe that what I was eating was not something that had been pulled live and coldly wriggling from the earth. At first. Now I, too, when I can get them here, keep small jars marked Leiden with me. It is lovely to hold a bit of herring in your mouth.

Steal something, he said.

First, tell me what's going on, I said, but halfheartedly, already caught up, even in those first moments, in the gears of the machine grinding away in Mr. Kindt's apartment.

Oh, but that would be so dreary, so boring. Steal something, Henry. Be a thief!

What should I steal? I asked him.

There are many things here worth stealing.

I looked around. I couldn't see very well.

Steal anything then get out then come back for dinner tomorrow evening, my dear young man.

Go to this address, Tulip tells me.

We've met. We've gotten friendly. We've shared a few drinks. Exchanged anecdotes. I've told her that in one of my recurring dreams, Death, dressed as a cabdriver eating a hot dog, rips me out of my shoes as I'm walking up Avenue B. She's asked me what I do when I'm not having bad dreams, and I've told her I'm a thief.

Go to this address and see the things this guy has.

Why?

Go there. It will be lucrative, she says.

I go there. Eighth Street, view of St. Brigid's and the park. Vintage real estate. I go up lots of stairs. The door is wide open. Mist or cold smoke billows out and I walk in.

TWO

Once upon a time I was someone then that stopped. Once upon a time I had a job and lived in an apartment on the Lower East Side, surrounded by the sounds of Dominican Spanish. Salsa music in the summer. The *whack-whack* of dominos. Old guys selling flavored ices for fifty cents on the corner. Bad engines revving up. In the afternoons and evenings, kids would stand in the broadening bands of shadow, slugging and kissing and laughing at each other, and in the mornings the streets were clogged with street sweepers and garbage trucks and soft-faced, groggy locals moving their cars. The buildings around me weren't nice, exactly, but they were old and kind of mysterious, with people leaning out of or moving behind the windows, and there were synagogues nearby and churches and a lot of small neon signs. The apartment I lived in was improbably large, with high ceilings and turquoise floors, and it looked out over an empty lot to a white wall, which represented, I sometimes thought as I stood at the kitchen window and looked over to it, whatever vanished building had once stood there full of bowls of ice cubes and electric fans and sweat pooling in the steaming creases of more or less happy or unhappy but now at any rate probably long-vanished skin.

There were cats in the apartment. Making a lot of racket. Breaking things. Laying their lazy asses around. They used to wake me up in the morning by attacking my feet. Biting and lifting off little bits of skin with their claws. But they were my cats and I enjoyed their ministrations, and the damage to my feet and to the basically pretty cheap glassware in the apartment was part of the domestic program. Carine didn't mind. There would be a flash of gray and a large glass object would hit the deck and shatter and she would light a cigarette and look at me with a dazzling violet gleam in her eye and shrug and smile. Carine. Small. Bones like a pepper finch. Elegant of arm and leg. Always carefully shod. She had a short bob haircut and vintage garments, a propensity to build up static charges, and the softest, palest skin. She used to like to quote the poets. After dinner in the East Village, out on the little terrace at Jules, the ashen air of St. Mark's Place shot through with street and cab light, seared by the softly burning faces of the people sweeping past. She would quote poets then drink heavily. We both did. "All the colors I could write are not fair as this," she would say. Glass after tannic glass.

She liked the cats, liked to comfort them, to comfort me. She'd had a cat she'd loved dearly during her time in France, and she liked my cats and would smear lavender-scented antiseptic cream into the claw marks on my feet. She would cradle my head in her lap on one of her soft black skirts when it wasn't too warm, and she would smoke little Mexican rice-paper cigarettes and tell me about the Ardèche, where she had spent a summer, and about the mist that hung over the Bois de Boulogne in the early morning after a long night out on the town in "Gay Paree." Sometimes she would make an enormous salade niçoise with fresh greens and olives and hard-boiled eggs and tuna and green beans and lots of Dijon mustard, and afterward, if the timing was right, if we had heard the sad, chirrupy song making its wobbly-tire way along the block, I would run down to the street and bring her back up a frozen vanilla custard with tangerine sprinkles from the Kustard King.

Then, whammo, one night and the next morning she'd left. Before long, after the phone had been cut off, people started pounding on the door. It would start early in the morning and end late at night. First it was friends. Then it was creditors. Eventually it was my landlord. I had never liked him. His idea of fixing something in a tenant's apartment, like a hole in the ceiling, was to offer to pay you for doing the work yourself. Then to offer to take it off your rent. Then to ask you what the fuck you were talking about when you brought it up with him. Lately he had started construction of a new building in the vacant lot outside our windows. First they smashed into the ground, really beat the shit out of it with their sledges and steam shovels and endless, deadly serious curses, then slowly, morning by horrible early morning, it began to grow, erasing the white wall as it moved skyward. When I figured I had about a week, a week and a half tops, of unencumbered white-wall viewing and concomitant old-time-tenement imagining before it had blotted out space and sun, I asked my landlord to step over to the window with me, put my hand on his shoulder, and told him he had ten seconds to apologize.

After that I had the place over the comic book store. With the cats, only now there was just one. She used to pull chip crumbs out of the bottom of the bag with her paw. It was a whole business. I'd sit on the bed and watch her. Offer her my foot but she had moved on—to chips and laundry detergent and a big black tom she hissed at through the window. Who was I with then? Can't remember. I read a lot of comic books and graphic novels, granted. A guy at the Dark Room, where I worked the door for a few weeks, lent me a beat-up copy of De Quincey's writings. My acquaintance was into the opium eater thing, which gave me shivers and made my head spin, but it was the long essay, "On Murder Considered as One of the Fine Arts," that grabbed me, that set me to dreaming.

Dreaming, I saw a fire down the block, stood too close to it for too long while they were putting it out, then smelled it on my clothes for days. This smell, though I wasn't quite sure why, repeatedly put me in mind of my aunt, sitting at home at the kitchen table, where I had last seen her, head down, barely moving. Once, I thought I saw her on the street below my window, and even though I knew there was no way it was her, I leaned out and started yelling. Then I was without lodgings for a time.

THREE

I stole a book.

He said to me, dear boy, you are a thief so steal something.

How do you know I'm a thief?

Because it is dark. Because you are in my apartment. Because I did not ask you to come. Because you have confessed to having taken the trouble at least to attempt to monitor my movements. Take something, then, perhaps, knock me down, then come back for dinner tomorrow night and we will talk.

What? I said.

He smiled, stood up with a rustling of plastic-coated wires, and gestured with his head toward all the things, the hundreds of things, that were in the room.

Come back tomorrow night at nine o'clock. I will feed you fish and we will talk.

Fish? I said.

With fine crackers. It doesn't matter whether you are on time or not.

You want me to come back? I said.

Yes, he said. But not to steal. That's only tonight.

You're inviting me to steal something from you.

Yes.

In other words, you're saying "take something."

He laughed his little crushed-lightbulb laugh and looked around the room.

All right, take something, Henry, he said. It's not difficult. The difficult part was walking through my door.

O.K., good, great, I said. I shrugged, and cracked my neck and three fingers to cover the fact that I felt equal parts spooked and intrigued, put my hand into the shadows and picked up the first portable item it touched, walked over and sort of shoved the item's owner a little on the shoulder so that he fell back with a light *oof* and a crinkling of wires into his big chair, then made for the door. When I got downstairs and out onto Eighth Street I took the time to confirm that what I had grabbed was a musty old book, which didn't smell very good. I'm not at all against reading, in fact I read a lot, but not books that smell like something that has spent time in one of New York's omnipresent mystery puddles. I tossed the book into the trash can next to the entrance to Tompkins Square Park, thought, well, that was pretty crazy, then went down to the Horseshoe, on the corner of Seventh and B and had a couple. Couple more. Thing is I'd done pretty well with a score I had made while I was in the hospital and I still had plenty in my pockets. Going to Mr. Kindt's had just been gravy and it didn't matter that I'd left without anything worth keeping. I asked the guy behind the bar—Job was his name—for a shot and told him to help himself.

Thank you, Job said.

You're welcome, Job.

We drank.

Two more, I suggested.

Job poured two more.

You ever feel spooked and intrigued, Job?

At the same time?

More or less.

I'm not sure.

I told Job about my encounter with Mr. Kindt.

Mr. what? said Job.

I hear you, I said.

Job grinned. He went off to help a couple of customers. He came back.

What's your real name, Job? I asked him.

Job's my real name.

I mean your name before it was Job.

Anthony.

Anthony's a nice name.

Might be, but it's not my name.

Fair enough.

Job moved off. I drank some more, then some more, and I thought about Mr. Kindt saying "dear boy," and I both liked it and I didn't, and I thought about seeing him naked and bathed in the green light, and wondered what it would be like to have all those wires attached to me. I shivered. For a second, I could remember having had wires attached to me, could remember my aunt leaning close with her roll of tape, her graying hair falling over her face, could remember the flecks of bacon fat on her chin. Actually, I had never had wires attached to me. *Remember* isn't the right word. Henry boy, sweet boy, I could "remember" my aunt saying. I shivered. I smelled fish and felt mist, then I was sitting in a booth and someone was whispering in my ear: five hundred dollars.

Sold to the drunk biped in the booth, I whispered back.

There's a little shop at Forty-eighth and Lex. Doesn't look like much on the outside. Ask for Mr. Singh. He'll give you five hundred dollars for it and that's if you don't feel like bargaining.

Tulip. Sitting close and spinning. For a second she looked a little like a pale yellow pinwheel, like the retinal afterimage of a fizzing golden firework. Only she was wearing gray and had on one of those aviator's hats, which completely covered her blond hair and set her eyes to sparking and crackling, so that what I should have been seeing in the money end of my similes was something opalescent, azure, electric blue.

Tulip, I said. I was just talking to Job.

The bartender? His name's not Job, said Tulip.

She was running her finger across the book I had tossed in the garbage can. It was sitting open on the table and there was a diagram of the interior of an arm. Vein system. Musculature. Old stuff. From back when surgery meant ugly things for everyone except the rats. Looking at it, I thought first of Manhattan and the deep hole that had been punched in it, then of this movie I'd seen in which a king had his arm operated on. He died. There was a long battle for succession. The country was laid to waste. Years passed. Hope began to glimmer in the east. The people prepared themselves. They set off on long marches and learned new songs. Then hope faded and the rats took over. I was guessing this book was about that old. It was written in Greek and Latin. Lots of significant-looking words. I tried to read one. No luck.

So what's his name? I said.

Anthony.

Good-looking guy.

I put my finger on some delicately articulated vein system, ran it down a leg. There were shadows everywhere. It was like I was back at Mr. Kindt's.

He was home. I watched him leave, but he was home anyway, Tulip. He was sitting there, naked. He told me to take whatever I wanted.

He's a little strange that way.

He was also hooked up to a heart monitor. He told me to steal something, then he invited me to dinner.

I know.

How?

Because I was there.

Where? In one of the big jars?

She laughed.

What's going on, Tulip?

Nothing, I told him about you and he wanted to meet you.

Why?

Because I told him he'd like you.

You set me up.

If you like.

How do you know him?

I just know him. A friend introduced me. She paused. She looked at, I think, something about her fingernails. Sometimes I do things for him, she said.

Things? I said.

She didn't answer.

I let it go.

Who is he? I asked.

An old guy, lonely, from upstate, but he's been in the city for years. I don't know. He's eccentric, he does some business.

I looked at Tulip. She was not smiling. I was drunk and didn't feel well. The bar was full of smoke and colored light.

I barely know you, Tulip, I said.

That's true, Henry.

How did we meet?

We met at a party.

Was it a good party?

We didn't stay.

We didn't go home together either.

No, we didn't.

What does he mean about fish?

He likes fish. Don't you like fish?

I thought about fish. I thought about the book, with its rotten puddle smell and stained pages and cross sections and strange diagrams.

Mr. Singh? I said.

She nodded, stood up.

I stood up. Or thought I did.

Good-night, Henry, I'm leaving now, she said.

FOUR

For a time, during this pre–Mr. Kindt period, while I was still presentable, I made inquiries about work. Simple, legitimate jobs. Ones that would have required me to lift or sweep or distribute small multicolored flyers, that would have given me the opportunity, in exchange for miniature paychecks, to don brightly colored clothing and hand food across the counter, or wear a hairnet and wash dishes, or fold freshly laundered clothes, or run a steam press, or wear a billboard advertising Optaline eye salve, but each time I went out my frame of mind quickly soured and I didn't have any luck.

One day, my mind already as sour as an old so-called SweetTart, I saw Carine as I was coming out of a hole-in-the-wall Indian deli on Roman Street with a day-old onion cake in my hand. I had meant to inquire about the position advertised in the window. Instead I had handed over fifty cents, scowled a little, and accepted the oily cake. Carine was wearing a handsome vintage gray suit and walking with her arm around a young man dressed in fashionably rumpled beige linen pants and a bright green Cockfighter T-shirt. I bit into the awful cake, chewed once or twice, then let it fall out of my mouth. Carine did not see me and I did not call out to her. She and her young man looked nifty together. I went back into the deli, asked about the job, and was immediately told I was "unsuited for the obligations." Chewing hard on the insides of my cheeks, I asked for my money back for the cake, scooped five gleaming dimes off the counter, then walked over to a lonely patch of wall on Eldridge Street, leaned back, shoved my hands into my pockets, saw a flickering procession of Carines in the handsome gray suit that I had helped her pick out the previous Christmas, and, with the taste of old onion and even older oil in my mouth, pretended, badly I imagine, that the substantial facial moisture that was threatening to bust loose was just something caught in my eye.

I beat someone during this period. Someone standing next to a deep fryer with grease flecks on his cheeks, who told me I smelled like I was dead and that I should get out and that I should not waste his time asking for work. He had a good life and he had worked hard for it and he had a feeling that *hard* and *work* were not words in my vocabulary. He spit in the sink after he said this.

I asked him if what he was saying, as someone else had recently said, was that I was "unsuited for the obligations." That I wasn't, in essence, up to the shit job he was offering for shit pay in his shit place.

He didn't answer. Instead, he repeated the thing about how awful I smelled.

You smell, baby, I said to him as I walked away, as he sat slumped against the refrigerator with his hands, palms up, at his sides.

I realize that divulging this kind of information about myself, whether or not it is true—some people I have told about it have looked at me and laughed, i.e., there may be some blur involved—does not help my position, but I can live with that. I have already, after all, been found guilty and sent here, and it is not my intention in chronicling the eventually unfortunate circumstances of my friendship with dear dead Mr. Kindt to sway public opinion. I was broke, and beat the shit out of someone, some jerk in the kitchen of an eating establishment, or I probably did, then laid low for a while. That's a fact.

By *laying low* I mean I got sort of swallowed up by certain parts of New York, not to mention certain events, and for quite some time wasn't presentable at all. The days and nights that compose this period seem now to have been poured into a bucket and tossed into the East River, so that every time I go looking for them it seems as if I am slipping out to sea. I know that at one point, when the gaping hole—in what I heard someone standing outside St. Mark's Church call "the arm of the city"—was still horrifyingly fresh, and the air was still stinging everyone's eyes, and you saw people going around like death's heads with their goggles and respirators on, I slept under some scaffolding on Great Jones Street in company with several others and that these several others didn't want me there. I also know that for a while I walked around with one eye swollen shut, because I can remember seeing my reflection in a mirror as I passed the shining windows of a Duane Reade. I can also remember, not very long after this, walking down my old street, late at night, looking up at my old apartment, where I could see a light and a little corner of the ceiling, and being overwhelmed by the feeling that I had slipped back into my old life, that Carine, with her gray suit and salade niçoise and soft lap, was upstairs with the cats. The feeling was so strong, or I wasn't, that I walked over to the door, reached into my pocket, felt for my keys, and was surprised not to find them. It seems to me it was at this juncture, as I reached with great certainty for something that wasn't there, that I felt the ground going out from under me and became convinced that I was looking for myself in my own pocket and that—this realization increased the size of the wave of disorientation that had swept over me—it was me, not my keys, that had been gone for weeks.

There were other moments—sitting in Battery Park eating the remains of a shrink-wrapped giant cookie, great clouds of smoke wafting out over the harbor, the Statue of Liberty gray instead of green and somehow, at least the way I remember it, lacking a face; or lying on a bench near the Cloisters, the unseasonably hot sun smashing me into a stupor, a man very nearly as unpresentable as I was walking over and pinching my arm.

He had a plan, he said, a wonderful plan that lacked only a partner. If I was interested in being that partner he would let me in on it. I told him I was interested. He said that before he could let me in on the plan he had to test me. I asked him what the test was. He said I had to find someone who looked like me and pinch him on the arm. I then had to tell him I had a plan and ask him if he would like to be my partner and, if he agreed, test him in the same way.

Your plan is to make people who are already dizzy even dizzier, I said.

It's not really my plan, he said.

All of this would no doubt have continued had I not, one night after I had swiped a bottle from a sleeping colleague and drunk half of it over a couple of Halcion, wandered out in front of a Gentle Fragrance Florists truck. This truck, even though it did little more than clip me, proved to be my ticket out. An ambulance arrived and strong arms put me on a stretcher and bore me away. I could see nothing out the ambulance windows—the world had been reduced to that bouncing over-lit interior and four small panes of dark glass. A man with a bored look on his face presided over my passage. I spoke at some length, but he either chose to ignore me or did not hear me or both.

In the hospital, I was bathed and fed and my dizziness receded. The food was served on flimsy pastel-colored trays and was pretty bland, but it was real and certainly more palatable than anything I had ingested in some time. In the hospital, I began to steal and to sell what I stole. In the hospital, I lay on a firm mattress and things happened.

FIVE

It was a little hard to figure out, once I became a regular at Mr. Kindt's, why Tulip was spending so much time with him. I mean for starters consider the physical discrepancy: Tulip young, tall, beautiful, with a penchant for tank tops and tight jeans and with long, fresh muscles that seemed to be living their own bright life beneath her simple clothes and the exposed expanses of her skin; old Mr. Kindt was beautiful too, but in the way that exotic mushrooms or worn-out manatees or bacteria formations are beautiful: a focus on certain aspects and angles is required. Of course, given some baseline commonalities and even, at times, without them, New Yorkers have a surprisingly high tolerance for dissimilarity, and I have no doubt that were I to rip the front off any of the buildings in, say, Stuyvesant Town, I would uncover a jaw-dropping proliferation of physical mismatches. So it wasn't so much that that confused me. It was something else, something about the way they were and *weren't* together, the way Tulip seemed practically to live there but also not to be there at all, the way Mr. Kindt would stare fixedly at her while seeming simultaneously oblivious to her presence, the way a troubling cocktail of ambivalence and affection seemed to sit at the heart of their interactions. Tulip was almost completely silent on the nature of and motivation for her relationship with our mutual friend. For his part, if asked about Tulip, and even if not asked, Mr. Kindt would offer up bon mots along the lines of: she takes care of me, the darling, or, I would be lost without her, the dear. The second one I wasn't so sure about, and the first one, despite my imaginings— which had started almost the moment she had told me she did "things" for Mr. Kindt—I quickly decided just wasn't true. Though she was awfully nice to have breathing in your direction as she sat cross-legged and barefoot in one of Mr. Kindt's overstuffed couches or armchairs, Tulip didn't particularly take care of anyone. Just about all she did for Mr. Kindt—at least that I was aware of—was hang around and help out with ambience and, occasionally, down in the little parlor on Orchard where she did some freelance work, give Mr. Kindt a tattoo. He had several, as I was to learn. They were rather intriguing. And certainly fit his general mysteries-and-perishable-properties-of-the-flesh aesthetic. I eventually got one too.

He had tiny blue eyes. He had a small head and a neck that looked like there was something wrong with it. Thick through the midsection, solid or had been, with stubby, hairless legs. So it was the eyes mostly, and it was his hands.

I soak them, he explained. You might consider it.

This was soon after I arrived, that second night. Tulip was there. Mr. Kindt was fully clothed. The heart monitor was sitting in a tangle of wires on a small table in the corner.

Look, he said, and, by way of demonstration, dropped his hands into a silver bowl with some kind of poorly mixed substance in it.

One hour a day, he said. Minimum. That allows the substance to seep in.

What is the substance?

Never mind, it's extraordinarily beneficial. Tulip, take the bowl away, please, he said.

It's true that Tulip did sometimes take Mr. Kindt's bowls away. It occurred to me after I saw her do this for the first time that regardless of whether or not I was witnessing one of the "things" she said she did, I was seeing something worth paying attention to. Believe me, it was far from unpleasing to watch—both as it was occurring and afterward—tall, lovely Tulip uncurl herself, come slowly forward, then walk across the room carrying a silver bowl.

He was a weirdo, basically. He was short and fat and was in the habit of wearing out everyone around him with his talk. He had been a quiver maker or something back in the old country and had had his tough times. A transformation of sorts had allowed him to break with his countrymen and, though it had not been easy, come to the United States. He had landed, still very young, in Cooperstown, upstate, where he had made certain acquaintances, who had helped him to acquire the stake that would transform his fortunes. This, he told me, had involved swimming the considerable length of Cooperstown's Lake Otsego on a bet.

Just like a fish, he said. An aquatic creature. In the Netherlands, my boy, I could swim all day and, when the weather was fine, all night. The gentlemen who told me I couldn't do it were afterward obliged to pull significant sums from both their literal and figurative wallets, prompting one of them to cry. They did not, of course, appreciate it when I handed them my handkerchief. It was really most remarkable.

Basically, he had done well and then better and had come to New York. Here, through hard work, luck, and a certain measure of ruthlessness, he had been able to acquire "many objects, many pretty things." One of his favorites, which I had a hard time understanding, was a hand-painted ceramic male duck, the green of whose feathers, he assured me, was most convincing. Another favorite, which hung on the wall in the kitchen beside the stove, was a framed daguerreotype of a young nun. The nun was in full nun regalia and was smiling. There was a kind of smudge over her right shoulder, like a messy thumbprint, which had been ascribed certain supernatural qualities of the prophetic variety. The smudge had apparently manifested itself during the developing process. No one had thought anything about it until on the very day the daguerreotype was brought home the young nun had been struck fatally on the right shoulder by a loose ceiling beam. Mr. Kindt told me he had a very handsome certificate somewhere, itself a clever counterfeit, that testified both to the veracity of the story and the authenticity of the daguerreotype. What pleased him most about his nun, he told me, was not the supposed mystical aspect of the image, but rather the early documentary evidence it provided of humankind's ongoing efforts to harness modern technology to aid and abet the most ancient variety of fraud.

Unchecked, he said, our belief systems eventually overrun everything, blot out the world, at the very least rewrite the map. That these belief systems are most often built on the model of the Indian mound—layer after layer of oyster shells, animal bones, and miscellaneous bric-a-brac: everything plus dirt—which grew, more or less blindly, ever upward and outward, until the people standing on it were either swallowed up or rolled off, seems only to underscore their authority in the minds of the initiated. History, it has been said, Mr. Kindt noted, is but the analysis of the impact of our systems, all of which glow with varying brightness for a time then grow dim.

Mr. Kindt liked to talk about history in this way and more than once offered different models for understanding it. One of my favorites was that history was simply love and destruction intermingled, their twin strands reaching far into the past, where a man or a woman, long since forgotten, inferred only through faint echo, stood grieving over one who had been lost.

Often when we were together we would munch on something. That first evening we munched on crackers and some kind of cold fish paste.

It's good, isn't it? he said.

Hmmm, I said.

There is a fine salt-to-oil ratio, is there not?

I thought about it. I didn't answer.

It is an acquired taste. You will acquire it.

I said I hoped so.

I am strange but you will get used to me, you know.

I looked at him.

Yes, you will get used to me.

I think, I said, I'm already starting to get used to you.

That's wonderful, my boy. But don't get used to me too quickly, otherwise you will get bored. So often, you see, they get bored.

They? I said.

A figure of speech, he said. He scooped a little paste out of the jar, daubed it onto a cracker, and handed it to me. My finger, in taking it, touched one of his. It seemed much softer than a finger should have been. When I had shoved his shoulder the previous night it had felt frail but normal. The substance, I thought. I shivered a little. His mouth made itself into a smile.

Contact, he said.

I took a bite of cracker and paste.

I'm not really much of a thief, I said.

Well, it was very nice of you to return that book, but I did really mean for you to keep it. By that of course I mean do what you wished with it. There is an excellent market in New York for such things.

So I heard.

I had brought it in with me and set it back in its place beside a tall cranberry-colored glass on a cluttered desk in a corner of the room. I do not in any way pride myself on maintaining standards of social decorum, but it did seem like pushing it a little to take someone's property, sell it, then go to his house for dinner. And over the course of the day, dinner with Mr. Kindt and, possibly, you see, with Tulip, had grown to seem quite appealing.

Where's Tulip?

Oh, she's around. She likes to wander, or nibble at things in the kitchen, or to lie down in the bedroom. She's a great one for lying down.

Mr. Kindt smiled.

I smiled.

Mr. Kindt took a bite of his own cracker and looked at me with his pretty little eyes.

She tells me you recently got out of the hospital.

I got hit by a truck. Broke a couple ribs and got banged up pretty nicely. I wasn't in very good shape to start with. I'm better now.

Tulip tells me you have some stitches.

On my head, you want to see them?

I started to lean forward and part my hair, but Mr. Kindt waved his hand and laughed.

Oh, but that's depressing, he said. Let's not look at your scar. I feel like talking. Ask me a question to get me going, ask me a question about history.

From the start, the idea of getting Mr. Kindt going struck me as vaguely alarming, but I try not to be, as a general principle, against alarming things. So with bits of cold paste coating the outer enamel of my teeth, I asked Mr. Kindt how he felt about, say, the purchase by the English of Manhattan from the Indians.

Excellent, Henry, that's an excellent question. It will allow me to speak about love and fish and history.

He rubbed his hands together, closed his eyes, opened them, and said, first of all, it was not a purchase, it was a loving exchange. Loving, *why*? you will say. What sort of word is *loving* in this context? It is *all wrong*—couldn't be more awful, or at the very, very least incorrect. But you see *loving* has many meanings. Loving is both the intricacy and the expanse. Loving is the tool that moves accurately through the flesh. Loving is the net that is moving forward and the sea that is contracting, the North Sea. Secondly, he said, leaning toward then away from me, it was the Dutch, not the English, who fucked over in such emphatically loving fashion the Manhattan Indians. It was the Dutch who founded New Amsterdam, who sailed their ships up and down the Noort Rivier, who traded in guilders, who swept patterns into the sand that covered their floors, who pined privately during the long hard winters for their land so far away across and below the sea.

When he finished, we ate some more paste. Tulip had returned. She sat there, legs crossed, the lamplight loving away at her cheekbones.

Now, *you* ask me a question, Tulip, Mr. Kindt said.

Tulip blinked slowly, looked at me, then at Mr. Kindt.

Not just yet, she said.

Any old question, said Mr. Kindt.

We're still digesting your last answer, Aris, Tulip said.

Is that right, my boy? said Mr. Kindt, looking at me.

I nodded.

It was intricate, I said.

Ah yes, which part?

The part about loving.

Well of course love is intricate, is the *most* intricate, is practically a synonym for intricacy. Of course *intricacy*—and as he said this he looked at Tulip out of the corner of his eye—has other synonyms.

Tulip leaned forward and took a cracker between two long white fingers.

O.K., she said. What do you mean by *intricacy*?

Ah, said Mr. Kindt. He grinned. He began to talk. He discussed the patterns followed by weavers, the "sinister" labyrinths of electricity and silicon that compose the microchips our culture "gobbles like salted peanuts." While he talked he moved around a great deal in his seat and waved his white hands through the air. Tulip looked very steadily in his direction the whole time he was talking, but I couldn't tell if she was listening or not. I knew I wasn't listening, at least not for part of it. And not because I didn't want to: I sort of did, I sort of liked it. It's just that for a couple of minutes, in between Mr. Kindt's discussing herring tissue and composite fibers and the putative chemical structure of evil acts, it all started to seem uncomfortably surreal—the paste, the broken-looking little guy who I'd seen naked the night before and who clearly liked to talk too much, the gorgeous woman sitting cross-legged on the couch in front of me, my presence there, possibly the codeine-enhanced painkillers I was still taking for my ribs—in a way that transcended the merely bizarre and actually started a couple of tiny alarm bells going off, and I had to fight back an urge to stand up and walk out of the room.

Which is what I should have done, of course, right then, and might have done, except that for some reason they both laughed and I found myself laughing, even though I wasn't sure what it was I was laughing about, and the tiny alarm bells stopped.

My dear boy, what would *you* be prepared to do under the aegis of love? said Mr. Kindt.

You mean in the same vein as what the Dutch so lovingly did to the Indians?

I mean it, of course, however you wish to take it.

I shrugged. I picked up something and put it in my mouth. I would do, you know, pretty much anything.

Give us an example of this "anything" you speak of.

You sure? I mean, there are a few different things that come to mind but they're all pretty elaborate.

We love elaborate, don't we, Tulip?

Tulip nodded.

O.K., I said. I told them about a scenario I had often entertained as a kid, involving a Jules Verne–type submarine that would take me to the bottom of the Mariana Trench, where I would disembark, in a special suit, and enter a grotto then a tunnel down which I would spelunk for miles, overcoming, as I went, multiple traps and numerous multilimbed ferocious-toothed guards, then pick or force the lock on the small iron door behind which my father was supposed to be kept, only he wouldn't be there. This would mean I would have to find my father's captor, force him, through awful means, including chopping one of his legs off, to tell me where my father was. He would tell me that my father was now being held on an off-world colony whose location was the highest secret. He would die laughing in my face. I would spend the next several years conducting an investigation that would take me all over the world in search of the secret to my father's whereabouts. I would finally get the answer in a bar made out of a shipping container on one of Jupiter's nastier moons. When I found my father, in a detention tower near the Sea of Tranquility, on Earth's moon, he would put his hand on my cheek and say, I knew you would find me, boy. I would pick him up in my arms. At that moment, my father's captor, mysteriously resurrected, would spring the trap he had been waiting to spring for years, locking both my father and me up together in the tower's chamber. There we would sit together and wait with no hope of rescue for certain death.

Some dark, end-of-the-galaxy sci-fi music would play in the background. We would be happy though. Together, with our arms wrapped around each other's shoulders or playing some game like Scrabble.

There was a silence after I had finished speaking. Mr. Kindt handed me another cracker and momentarily placed one of his unsettlingly soft hands on my knee.

My father died when I was ten, I said. He worked construction. Mostly housing, on Staten Island. I was raised by my aunt. It was a long time ago. He liked Scrabble.

Of course, Mr. Kindt said.

That wasn't the happiest "anything" scenario I could have come up with.

Happy, said Mr. Kindt. He made an exaggeratedly dismissive face and shrugged.

What would you do, Tulip? I asked.

I would do the same, of course, with the appropriate adjustments, she said. I might, for instance, go after my loved one, fight my way through the meanies, in a yellow submarine.

Mr. Kindt smiled. And I would set off in a purple diving bell, he said. One *should* do anything, yes, my dears.

The three of us sat quietly for a while then. It occurred to me that maybe this talk and cracker eating was all the dinner I was going to get, which was just fine with me. After all it isn't every night you get to talk about love and intricacy and herring, much less substances and oceans and swept floors. The truth is, once I had stopped feeling for those few moments like I had to immediately vacate the premises, had stopped wondering what the fuck I was doing there and the alarm bells had fallen silent, it all started to seem kind of cozy—the crackers, the anything scenarios, Tulip, Mr. Kindt, me.

At some point a bottle of brandy was brought out. Glasses were poured. Refilled.

Mr. Kindt spoke some more—about smoke and history. Looking in my direction, he said nice things about those we have lost, those who have vanished like so much dew on the oak leaves or something. At this I started to feel guilty and told him that in fact my father, as far as I knew, was still very much alive, that he had been and probably still was a construction worker, but that he had not died when I was ten. Until he had left for good he had come home most nights smelling of sweat and concrete and, after arguing with his sister, my aunt, who had taken over when my mother left not too long after I was born, had watched TV with me.

Ah well, the truth, Mr. Kindt said, in much the same way he had said "happy."

It was a good story, Tulip said.

Involving meanies, I said.

The best kind, my dear boy, Mr. Kindt said.

We settled into our chairs. The brandy took hold and the lights seemed to dim. Several weeks went by.

SIX

In my room there was one large window and across the window was what I took to be a bird net, but the whole time I was there I never saw a bird go by. Once in a while I saw balloons though. Floating up past the window, up past the black net. It wasn't hard to imagine where they came from, those metallic pink, blue, and yellow, I think, balloons: a small man next to a helium tank. He would have dozens of balloons, and it was far from inconceivable that occasionally after handing one to a child or a friend of a patient, even very carefully, it would slip free. The small man would look up at the sky then at his client then reach for another balloon. On the house, of course. That night, when he got home, his wife, dressed in worn high heels and holding a plastic tumbler, would ask him how he had done. It would take him a while, maybe a swallow or two of his wife's drink, before he admitted that he had been "forced" to do another two-for-one, which had cut into the day's profits. She would scold him halfheartedly, then fix him a drink, ask him to describe the child in question, and tell him she would have done the same. This balloon salesman scenario, which was a little different each time it came to me, was the explanation I settled on, although I was never able to confirm it. At any rate, the sight of the balloons put me in mind of my earlier days, specifically the fact that it used to please me greatly as a child, as I suppose it pleased many others, to ingest the helium of balloons and to talk. It used to please me, as it might have those many others, to say, fuck you, Mississippi. Try it and you will see why. I remember several times being disappointed that ingesting helium did not, in addition to making my voice sound so interesting, render me buoyant. Helium did, I suppose you could argue, provide me with a cast for my left arm that several of my fellow fifth graders signed and drew on with brightly colored markers. One of these illustrations was of what its artist, one Eva Grace Cotrero, explained was a moon lamp, a device she was working on that was supposed to promote healing by harnessing moonbeams. There was also a stick-figure drawing of Conan waving his Cimmerian steel sword, but it was much more difficult, because of its placement, to see. My friends wanted to know what it was like to jump off a shed roof. I told them what the doctor had told me: that it was like being a coconut and cracking your shell.

I saw a guy really crack his shell once. West Twenty-second Street. Ninth floor. Guy just looked both ways and jumped. No yelling. Didn't even kick his feet. Just fell. Big coconut. I told Job, the night nurse, that I had heard him hit the ground.

Job said, yeah?

Yeah, I said.

Only this wasn't Job. This was the doctor.

Hello, Doctor, I said.

How are you feeling today? asked the doctor.

Just fucking fine, I said.

The doctor was young and Dutch and didn't mind if I swore. At least up to a point and depending on the context.

From Amsterdam she was. Apparently she had a green card and was just months away from getting naturalized.

You know, a professional degree and connections, she said.

That still works even in this climate of international mistrust and general unproductive uncertainty? I said.

Apparently, she said.

She also said things like, no, your case does not trouble me at all, and, yes, I have had experience with similar cases, and, don't worry, you are progressing very, very nicely.

I don't want to progress, I said.

It's not productive to speak that way, Henry, she said.

She was tall and skinny and had blond hair pulled back up over her ears. They were nice ears. I used to mainly focus on them when she would come in. They were very small and looked like little curled-up hands, like what you see sometimes in reproductions of those in utero sonograms. Sometimes I was just lying there and wasn't in any state to do much of anything, and sometimes the doctor would lean over me to do something and then I could see her ears up close. Once I tried to reach up and touch one. Or thought I did. It danced and spun just out of reach of the hand I thought I was holding up to it. She had excellent teeth, too. I told Job this. Job concurred. He said that yes the doctor did have nice fresh-looking choppers, and nice pink gums for that matter. She was one healthy-looking customer. Looked like she could take apart a couple of nice raw steaks without burping. Like she could really rip them up. It was little wonder they were letting her stay.

We then talked for a time about teeth and gums. Mainly his and mine.

I won't show you mine, I said.

I'll pull back your lips and look after you've had your meds and you're asleep, he said. Do you want to sleep now?

Are you going to pull my lips back and look?

Yes.

I thought about the morphine hitting my system, about following it off down into the orange-colored depths, about going deliciously, temporarily blank.

O.K., hit me, I said.

Job hit me. Nice and hard.

I'm not sure how long I was initially scheduled to spend in the hospital, but I am now in a position to affirm that anything approximating a reasonable interval has long since elapsed. It is possible that relevant information was provided to me at some point and that I may well have it somewhere, maybe over on the shelf in the little armoire they've given me, but if it's there I don't know what it says. I do know, as I've mentioned, that time has passed and that I often, after receiving an injection, after the appealing aforementioned heat and blankness, dream. Many dreams—most dull, some not, a few of which recur. In one of them, which sometimes follows the nasty dream involving the cabdriver, I suddenly wake and the room, which is my room, is filled with wind and the wind is talking and what it is saying is not nice. The wind is not nice, and it howls around me, and talks and whispers, and I am on my bed awake and can't move. Or I am standing, say, in the center of the kitchen, and I can't move and there is no wind, but there is something there, something that doesn't like me. But mainly I am flat on my back in my bed, and I am awake and can't move, and there is the wind. There is the wind, and it talks and I can't move and I am flat on my back in bed. It is cold, and I am frightened. Sick.

In the meantime, anyway, when I wasn't dozing deep in my fine hospital pillows, which I did a lot, or being injected by Job or one of his colleagues, I watched TV, perused back issues of *National Geographic* and *Scientific American,* and picked through some of the books that floated around the waiting rooms. Most of them were standard mystery/thriller/romance fare that left me pretty cold. One, though, was a book of stories about a character with an unpronounceable name who gets up to all kinds of fascinating adventures in the far reaches of the galaxy or on the earth before dinosaurs had set up their shop or on the moon when it was still supposedly possible to make a day trip there. These stories reminded me of my interest, when I was a child, in telescopes, and of peering through them— even when they were broken, for example in old junk shops, or had their caps still on in the fancy stores—at whatever night sky full of dazzling lights and shimmering creatures that I could conjure up in my mind. Another book that I did more than pick through was a sad, strangely appealing narrative written by an author of the Germanic persuasion. My interest in this one can likely be attributed to the narrator's bizarre interests and the highly tenuous quality of the causalities he implied. On one half page, for example, a piece of silk would be torn and on the next a whole forest would be knocked down. Also, the narrator was always being hospitalized or talking about other people who were and things were just generally going to pieces. My favorite section of the book was about beautiful gold and ruby Chinese dragons, how when they rolled over, deep within the earth, seas went dry and mountains crumbled. I told Job about this part, then read it to him, and he said, yeah, and looked out the window, and said, I get that.

Once or twice, in the early days, they brought injured fire- and policemen into the hospital for treatment and cheers went up. I did not see these people being brought in, just extrapolated them from the cheering once I had been told, the first time, what the cheering was about. Everyone of course cheered fire- and policemen in those early days, even if their injuries were not directly related to the events downtown. I cheered them too, from my bed, even deep within the windy vagaries of my evening morphine, probably even, several times, when there were none of them around. But mainly, in the hospital, it was tv and magazines and books and consultations and medications. I.e., routine. It was this routine, and my growing familiarity with the staff and their patterns of movement, and the fact that one of the cabinets down the hall had a faulty lock on it for a short period of time, that eventually allowed me to steal a few things that I was able, through Job, to sell.

I don't do this regularly, Henry, said Job, after I'd passed on a few choice articles to him one night.

Me neither, I said.

I got a guy, said Job, makes everything easy. But I only see him once in a while.

I'll let you handle it.

Yeah, that's right. I'll handle it. And, Henry, they catch you and you start singing, you're just some homeless guy with a dent in his head, correct?

Mum's the word, Job.

That's right.

Except that, Job . . .

Yeah, Henry?

You didn't really put that too nicely.

You're right, I'm sorry. I was trying to make a point and got carried away—like I say, I don't do this very often, obviously I need to work on my technique.

You do.

I know.

I'm not just some guy—I mean, no one is just some guy. I used to have a girlfriend, you know.

I know. You told me.

So I slipped a little, I said. So I got lost. We've all got a little maze upstairs. We all take a wrong turn sometimes and end up who knows where, shivering in the shrubbery.

Now, there you lost me.

Are you being funny?

No.

I'm paraphrasing. It's from the book.

What book?

This book I'm reading. *The Rings of Saturn*. The one with the dragons. Whatever. What I'm thinking right now is that the dent in my head could be a lot bigger, correct? It could be an unplanned hole. A place to put a fist. A cup holder. An ashtray.

Job let me go on a little bit longer then smiled, put a hand on my arm, gave it a hard squeeze, and told me to can it.

I smiled back and canned it.

I liked Job, very much actually. Not least because of his tendency, not always intentional, to slip into passable Edward G. Robinson imitations when we were discussing business. He also had an excellent low-grade sense of humor, especially about other patients, and was willing to listen to everything I had to say about the doctor, often offering me humorous advice along the lines of, you should just come out and ask her for a xerox of that ear. Probably, of course, this isn't funny unless you have some morphine in you. Or maybe it is anyway, I don't know.

Sometimes, late at night, Job would sit by me as the evening meds nestled into the soft and secret areas of my brain and whisper strange little things or seem to whisper them as my eyes went shut. In this way, and in the ways I have just described, the early days and nights passed.

SEVEN

Mr. Kindt liked the museums. He liked the marble on the floor and the possibility of grand staircases and the displays so brightly and evenly spaced. He liked the statues with the arms snapped off and the small ivory carvings and the ancient bone-and-wood playing boards and the skeletons comparatively displayed. He liked the thick glass, with its "strange, dissipated reflections." He liked the roped-off areas and the animals made of plastic and clay. He liked the displays with sounds and the possibility of narration. He had often wished, he said, he could play a substantive role in the creation of the text for these narratives and wondered how well his voice would be suited to high-quality recording. He liked the short explanatory notes by the exhibits, which he said were "like funereal inscriptions," and he liked the proximity of dead languages, and the juxtapositions of artists and the guards and monitors and checkpoints. He liked the people moving slowly and silently, and the art holding its position, absolutely still.

Look at *that,* he liked to say in the museums. He liked to say, ah, yes, this one, or, compare this one to that one, or, just, ah . . . He liked to bend, carefully, and to straighten, slowly, and to hold out his hand and to take it away. Mr. Kindt always wore his hat in the museums. For that matter, with rare exceptions, he always wore his hat in the house. It was a black felt hat with a large floppy brim. He liked that kind of hat. He liked, in fact, for me to wear a similar hat, a black job with a slightly smaller brim, which he handed me one day when I walked through the door.

Uh? I said.

Would you, Henry, my boy?

It wasn't so bad because Tulip also had a hat, floppy and black. Although it wasn't quite as stylish as the aviator's hat, the fringe of spun gold falling in sheets from the dark felt was, as Mr. Kindt put it one afternoon as we ate sliced hard sausage, pâté, and leftover meatloaf prior to going out, a truly noteworthy sight.

So the three of us would sit there at the table or would stand there in the museum. With meat in our mouths. Chewing in the yellow light. Or not chewing, no meat, at the American Museum of Natural History, in front of the Animals of the Plains exhibit—a life-sized diorama with stuffed grazing animals and a stuffed carnivorous animal and a painted background behind glass. Tulip especially liked the next diorama over—the Displaced Animals in Urban Environments exhibit—which showed a flock of cherry-head conures perched in a tree next to a wooden balcony where some long-ago shellacked seed had been spread. Painted on the curved wall behind them was a broad-stroke rendition of San Francisco, with the bay off in the distance. A pair of the conures had been frozen in what was supposed to be midflight, but this potentially dynamic touch hadn't been carried off as successfully as it could have been. A number of the birds that weren't focused on the seed had their heads cocked to the left and were peering skyward, presumably, we decided, at the tiny painted hawk circling far overhead. After we'd stood there a minute, Tulip spotted a conure with a blue head nestled in a spray of bright orange trumpet flowers. The explanatory note, which Mr. Kindt conjectured had been assembled in haste, made no mention of this handsome aberration. It spoke only of the redheaded variety that was "already several generations into its stay in the wilds of San Francisco." Apparently the "wilds" of New York were also home to an unnamed variety of nondomesticated parrot, although they had not been quite as successful as their cousins by the bay. Seeing an opportunity to draw Tulip out, I made some light remarks about birds, flapped my arms a few times to demonstrate what it was I thought was off about the conures that were supposed to be caught in flight, then asked her why she liked this display so much. Instead of answering me directly, she took Mr. Kindt's arm, dabbed at her upper lip with the pointed end of her tongue, and said to both or neither of us that after the events downtown she had seen a very large parrot with a yellow head vanish into the haze over the water near Battery Park.

Perhaps the most beautiful of the exhibits in the museum was the Hall of Planet Earth. Here there were sulfur chimneys from the floor of the ocean and zircon crystals from near the beginning of time. Mr. Kindt stopped and stood for a long while in front of the display on tectonic displacement and even longer in front of the garnets set in black granite pulled out of the heart of the Adirondacks, a range he was fond of because of its many streams and lakes. An illuminated globe on the ceiling demonstrated the effects of drastic climate change, and Mr. Kindt sat so long on the circular recessed benches under it, watching the clouds vanish and the continents go brown and the oceans evaporate and the reverse of this process, that Tulip and I fell asleep. I woke, I thought, to Mr. Kindt whispering in my ear: it was like that, it will be like that; and to Tulip, her eyes glinting in the reflected light of the barren continents, looking at me.

Or we would go to the movies. Mr. Kindt liked the old films. The black-and-white ones with all their "precise inaccuracies," with all their instances of exaggeration for the purposes of evoking artifice and, for the same reason, settings that were not quite right.

It is the almost-world I have so often dreamed of, Mr. Kindt said one afternoon as the credits rolled on a film in which a man and a woman had walked for fictional hours through a fabric jungle. The world that all these so-called realist films we have today have banished from the screen. Imagine, my dears, if we could forever slip, or, more important, feel ourselves slipping, like the floodlit ghosts of those old actors and actresses, from one happily constructed world to another, rather than, as we flesh-based units are obliged, from inexplicable light to inexplicable gloom.

Sometimes, if the theater was crowded, we would take our hats off and fan ourselves with them. We would sit there, the three of us, or the two of us if Tulip hadn't come, and the mouths on the walls of light would move and the sound would come out of the walls and our hats would move back and forth in front of us like instances of pure darkness that looked lost in the brightness that lit our faces in sporadic bursts.

Mr. Kindt liked to sit in the front row. He liked, in look-ing up at the screen, he said, to have to arch his neck, and he liked for his neck, as a reminder, he said, to have to hurt.

Reminder of what? I asked.

Of my namesake, he said.

Your namesake? I said.

But he didn't answer.

Sometimes, as we watched, I would let my hand move behind Mr. Kindt's pale white neck and I would allow my fingers to exert a certain amount of pressure that Mr. Kindt, his desire to have his neck hurt notwithstanding, loved.

It was this deep enjoyment of orchestrated experiences in which pain and pleasure lay tightly coiled that had prompted Mr. Kindt, I presumed, to take out a membership at the Eleventh Street Russian baths, a venerable mobster-frequented establishment where what I took to be blast fur-naces filled with boiling, beet-red lumps of flesh coexisted with sinister massage cabinets and a deep icy pool. Because of a recent change in management policy, a coeducational sweat-extruding experience was available most days, mean-ing both Tulip and I could accompany Mr. Kindt and par-take with him of his biweekly round of steams and saunas and lashings with oak leaves. It was Mr. Kindt's rule, one that Tulip and I were both happy to comply with, that if we went with him we did all of it. So it was that, to my surprising delight, I had a huge guy sit on my back, soap me up, whack me with oak branches, and time and again pour near-frozen water on me. Also, of course, I got to witness Tulip, who was built even more extraordinarily than I have helped you to imagine, in a wickedly petite

gold-and-green bikini, receiving the same. It was also plea-
surable, though differently, less dramatically, to watch Mr.
Kindt—in part for the blissful smile that would spread over
his mottled features as he was being smushed and swatted,
in part for the gleam, through the dim, burning air, of his
little blue eyes. So it was, anyway, that after changing into
bathing suits, over which, at the start of each session, we
draped a sort of house-issue smock, we went down into the
steamy gloom of the baths and moved together from one
area to the next, a progression that always ended with a col-
lective shriek in the pool of ice water and a race, well, a
race between me and Tulip, back upstairs.

Sometimes we went out to eat. When Mr. Kindt wasn't at
home he liked variety in his dinners, which meant we split
time between North African, Thai, Chinese, Japanese, and
Indian. Mr. Kindt's preferred Indian establishment was a little spot on the corner of First and Sixth. The tiny dining
room was festooned to the point of feeling overrun with
garlands of flashing red lights that were reflected, in ever-
receding depths, by panels of glossy plastic and hand-cut
disks of wrinkled foil. Mr. Kindt, who was well liked by
the staff for his generous tips, loved the minuscule tables
and the jostling of the waiters and the 3-D wallpaper and
the accelerant effect all this had on the complex combinations of tastes and smells. "Cardamom diffused throughout
a blend of lamb and cream and good Bengal curry is
magnificent, but cardamom diffused throughout a blend of
lamb and cream and good Bengal curry under blinking
Christmas lights is sublime" being the sort of remark he
was apt to offer us or the waiter or even fellow diners.

Mind your fucking business, the larger and more aggressively postured of a pair of young men sitting at a table near us said one evening after Mr. Kindt had directed a like observation in their direction.

Pardon me, gentlemen, but you *are* my business, Mr. Kindt said.

Both young men slowly turned their heads toward Mr. Kindt.

Then both young men flinched.

Oh . . . , the smaller of the two said.

Not to worry, Mr. Kindt said. The two of you will leave now and when you leave I will put money on your table to pay for your abrogated dinner. How was your abrogated dinner? I hope that you had time to enjoy one or two bites before you addressed yourselves so unpleasantly, so gratuitously, to me.

We should have known better, the larger one said.

Yes, you should have known better, so good-night, boys. Good-night, boys, and don't fucking come back, Mr. Kindt said.

When the two of them had left, Mr. Kindt reached over and put some money on their table. He also took a piece of their untouched chicken tikka and put it on Tulip's plate.

Everywhere we went, Mr. Kindt paid. He always had a tremendous amount of cash with him and he was not averse to slipping a couple of twenties into my pocket at the end of an evening before I went home. After a while, I asked Tulip about this, and if she thought Mr. Kindt was expecting a little something in return.

He's just generous, she said.

Right, I said.

She smiled.

Why don't you ask him what he wants? I don't know.

I did. It was evening, and he had just been showing me something about the lights in Tompkins Square Park from his window, how "lovely and scattered" they were, especially through the black netting, like some kind of "sparkling sea creature," or maybe, I said to myself, not really getting what he was trying to show me, like a sparkling sea creature that has been blown to bits. We were still standing there, gazing, when I said, Mr. Kindt, is there anything you would like me to do for you?

He looked up at me.

How do you mean, Henry?

I mean you've been very generous.

Have you been enjoying yourself?

Sure. Yes—absolutely.

Well then that's perfect.

So there's nothing I can do for you?

You can get Tulip off my bed and tell her it's time to eat.

I looked at Mr. Kindt.

I meant I could help you, if you needed it, with your business engagements, or with, you know, anything you want.

Mr. Kindt took my arm. He held it for a moment in one of his cold little hands then let go and gave it a few pats.

Don't worry about my business affairs, they are quite well looked after, such as they are at this late stage in my career, my boy, he said. As far as anything else goes, I am an old man and like to talk and I do not like to talk alone. Tulip has been a wonderful companion to me, but it occurred to both of us that another friend might be even more wonderful, and now we are fortunate to have you. It is certainly true that, on occasion, friends do things for each other, but for now I'm not sure what it is exactly besides rousing that lovely wisp of a Tulip you can do.

I looked at him.

He looked at me.

All right, sure, I said.

EIGHT

The early, the innocent, the unambiguous days and nights in the hospital gave way to an indeterminate period during which I thought I had received my discharge orders and returned to the world of cars and bricks and clogged gutters—where things went well then badly then worse— but then I was back or had never left, I had never left, there I was, and in the deep and dark hours of the night I woke from the dream of wind and voices and met an old man.

May I call you Henry? he said.

Yes, of course, I said.

My name is Aris Kindt.

I saw you today when they were looking at your throat are you sick they tell me I'm not well but I'm better what's wrong with you? I said.

I know, he said.

What do you mean, you know?

His upper lip curled a little. He shrugged.

Well, Mr. Kindt, may I call you Mr. Kindt, then you also know that I'm a thief—that I'm thieving in this establishment, that I'm making a fucking killing. And speaking of fucking, I wouldn't mind, that is, with my doctor, she's a peach, a pale yellow one with funny ears, do you know her?

My throat is fine, he said. It's much better. Thank you for asking.

Your throat?

His lip curled again.

Dr. Tulp, I said. Best thing about this place, very bright, an incandescent bulb, a light-emitting diode. She's getting a green card. She likes me a lot, takes my case very seriously. I'm in her office all the time. My humble room here is her second home. Peaches. I grew up on Long Island. Well, Staten Island too. That's my story. My father was in construction. Do you know Job? We're in business. We're practically fucking partners.

Shhh, he said, putting a hand on my shoulder. That's the morphine talking. It often talks much louder than is necessary about things not everybody need hear. I haven't even properly introduced myself yet—we can allow a greater measure of detail into our discussions after I have done so. Does that sound like a good idea?

It does, I said.

I went quiet. I closed my eyes. When I woke again he was gone.

He reappeared the next night and sat very still for a long time. We stared at each other and then he went away. He came back minutes or hours later with a large red balloon and asked me if I wanted a bite.

I nodded and he brought the balloon close to my mouth. It bobbed in front of my face. I shook my head.

There is less morphine in you now than there was earlier, certainly less than there was last night, he said. He ate his balloon, very slowly, very neatly. It didn't pop, just grew smaller, bite by careful bite. When he was finished, he said, we have things in common, young thief, then he went away.

He came back near dawn.

What do you want? I said.

Listen, dear Henry, and I'll tell you. May I?

I nodded. He crossed his legs and wrapped his hands around his knee. He cracked his neck loudly then began speaking.

Once upon a time, he said, there was a man who lived in a large Dutch town in the center of drab, flat farmland, where he had been obliged to do day labor as a child and to eat all manner of foul things, which were advertised as fresh and healthy and were neither. The man had grown up to become a maker of inexpensive quivers and had been bad at it and had married unsuccessfully because that was the sort of luck he had so he became a thief. He stole scrap iron from a blacksmith to sell to a cooper and flour from a baker to sell to local housewives. He stole three copper coins from an apothecary and a bolt of blue silk off the back of a milliner's cart. He stole eggs and whole cheeses and bundles of hops and once the corpse of a foal, which he attempted to sell for its hooves. For a long time he was unable to rid his mind of the smell of the rotting foal, even though he had tied a rope to it and dragged it well behind him. Then he got run out of town. He was not hurt badly, but was badly scared and was nervous around open fire for the brief remainder of his days. For a time he wandered. Autumn gave way to brutal winter. After knocking about at loose ends for some weeks he ended up in Amsterdam. In Amsterdam, his luck went from poor to very bad. A woman he groped at one night took his purse and left blood dripping from his right eye. The next day he attempted to knock someone down and to steal this someone's cape. He had been drinking. A kind of potato spirit. Very potent. He had procured a large knife, a jagged, rusty job with a bad handle. What he attempted to do was not what he did. His efforts were approximate. The someone he attempted to knock down and whom he had slightly wounded with the knife, the handle of which had crumbled during the attack, was a magistrate. Not a great magistrate. Not the magistrate behind door number one or two, the magistrate behind door number four or five, but still, a magistrate, and a vigorous, broad-shouldered one at that, who got up, flung down our drunken thief, and promised, through clenched teeth, to deliver him to justice. He was duly arrested, beaten, tried, hung. Within hours, perhaps as an extension of his punishment, his corpse was taken to the Waaggebouw, a medical amphitheater, where, before an audience of Amsterdam's finest citizens and foreign guests, possibly including such luminaries as René Descartes and Sir Thomas Browne, it was opened and sectioned with a scalpel and a number of fine saws. Rembrandt, who was also in attendance that day and made sketches, later immortalized the event in one of his most famous paintings, *The Anatomy Lesson*. Are you familiar with that painting?

I think so, I said.

I'm sure you know it. I'll have to see if I can put my hands on a reproduction, there are some very faithful ones available. Of course these widely available reproductions lack texture and ruin the colors, but they will give you the idea, put across the gist.

I'd like that, but . . .

But why, my dear Henry, am I telling you this?

I nodded.

You should sleep now, he said. You are not well and I've troubled you enough.

No trouble at all, I said.

That's very nice of you to say, but still, I should go.

Before you do, why don't you tell me what it is you think we have in common?

Mr. Kindt looked at me with his pale blue eyes. He licked his lips and leaned closer.

What we have in common is that we're both thieves, Henry. Not terribly successful ones.

NINE

New York is swell. It is swell on a cold wet night and it is
swell on a cold clear dawn. It is swell with the cars coming fast toward you and it is swell down by the subway
tracks, where the people come to gather and watch each
other and wait. It is swell with the attractive denizens and
with those who are not, including those, like you, who
might once have been. It is swell with the shop lights and
it is swell with its skyscrapers and acres of rubble and brilliant glass-strewn streets with everyone loving everything
and moving through the haze of airborne particles saying
fuck you. It is swell with its parks and harsh, windswept
open spaces, with its beautiful giant bridges, with its great
river and grim estuary, its cardboard villages, its scaffolding,
its doves in the morning, its sparrows and pigeons and
hawks and wild parrots basking in the sun. Its layers of
sonic and visual complexity are swell. Swell too is the little girl screeching with delight on the carousel at Bryant
Park, while the cars go by, bits of garbage flick through the
air, the wind irritates the trees, chairs are scraped again and
again over gravel, the ground rumbles distantly as the trains
plow the dark tunnels, grackles fight, small, unseen electric
explosions, wrecking balls, gobs of spittle smacking the
pavement, someone claps, someone taps the Gertrude Stein
statue on the shoulder, someone stumbles on an abandoned

bright pink beauty-company supply case. Astoria and Fort Greene and Hell's Kitchen and Spanish Harlem and Washington Heights and Cobble Hill are swell. Swell, as we have already seen, are the museums, movies, bathhouses, and restaurants frequented by petty hoods. A woman says, where are they all going? Another slaps her Bible shut. A man groans a little as he stoops to pick up a weather-stained pamphlet from the Church of Scientology. Two boys dressed in identical oversized Knicks jerseys take turns kicking a plastic Yoo-hoo bottle and doing beautiful 360-degree jumps over every crack. New York is unbelievably swell with its loud surfaces and sharp, sweeping contours, even more so with its endless peripheral zones. There people are told to hush or leave, to stand with their faces pressed against wet brick, to back away slowly, to curl up in a ball, to pay for that hot dog, to hand over a few bucks for a little New York City porn. You get, say, five minutes, and you open the magazine you've chosen and you've got this guy and another guy and three gals and some objects or you've got this gal and this gal and maybe a table and some green underwear or maybe a couch and a guy and a magazine or a guy with big hair and bad features wearing bell-bottoms, holding a book, listening to a "hi-fi," and a young gal wearing a cream-colored fur-lined negligee enters stage left looking surprised and even more surprised, in the next panel, when the guy is standing and opening his pants.

New York is swell, you think, as you leave the brightly lit shop, warmed in the body though not in the heart, and get back onto the glittering, grimy street. As you walk toward the neon billboards and giant television screens of Times Square you think about New York's swellness in almost cosmic terms, wondering where it begins and where it stops, and what is all that why in the middle, and then you leave off thinking and are just walking, past face after face backed by stone, steel, and dark brick, down into the subway and then out again at Fourteenth and First, where your mind flicks back on and you realize you just spent five bucks in a porn shop looking at what now seem like grotes-queries, pure and simple, and that you're broke and hun-gry and that, even though things have been much better lately, even though New York is so swell in so many ways, things are still far from perfect, far from soothing, far from, moment to moment, ideal. So you head over to see Mr. Kindt, your dear friend, who often feeds you, who often talks to you at great length about not uninteresting things, who frequently eases the pain of parting, now that you have exhausted your own supply of funds, at the end of the evening. Mr. Kindt, who greets you at the door on this par-ticular night, this night that is now in question, before you've even rung the bell and who says to you, come in, come in, Henry, I'm so glad you decided to drop by. It feels like it has been ages. What on earth have you been up to? Was it just the day before yesterday that you accompanied me to Russ and Daughters? There is a little of the pickled whitefish left and some dried pears. You can take it with you later. Where have you been? Never mind. I'm so happy to see you. Your timing couldn't be more perfect. Mr. Kindt, who says, you see, I would like, this evening, to introduce you to a murderer.

A murderer? you say.

He has ushered you into the front room. There is some unfamiliar outerwear hanging on the eighteenth-century cherrywood coatrack. You hear voices. You go into the living/dining room, Mr. Kindt's hand on your elbow, his breathing a little louder than usual. A small man with gray hair, deep wrinkles, and large, indistinct features turns toward you.

Here he is, says Mr. Kindt.

Hello, you say.

Hello, says the murderer.

He cordially shakes your hand and asks you how you do and you tell him that the day has been difficult for various reasons, but, as is always the case when you walk through Mr. Kindt's front door, things have improved.

I know exactly what you mean, says the murderer.

You are both too kind, but there is really no need, says Mr. Kindt.

Then you eat, the four of you, no, the five—you, plus Mr. Kindt, plus Tulip, plus the murderer, plus the murderer's guest, who is just returning to the room from the toilet with a cell phone pressed against her ear. She is a knockout. She is almost as tall as Tulip, has gorgeous mahogany skin, broad shoulders, and mile-long legs, and is bald. She slips her tiny phone into an orange shoulder bag.

I hope it's all right, she says, not to you but to Mr. Kindt. I've asked a friend to join us.

Mr. Kindt does not mind. He says as much and smiles, and when he smiles his little blue eyes are sucked back into his face and his rather bad but not unsightly teeth are exposed. He waves his hand over the bowls of nuts and olives and cubed Gouda that are spread out over the table. He says, we will just nibble and chat until they get here.

We nibble and chat. The knockout tells a story about a cab that almost ran her over and how she took off her heels, chased it down at the next light, and smashed out one of its rearview mirrors with a rock. You don't believe a word of the story but admire the way she tells it, punctuating her sentences with the brisk ingestion of carrots and cheese cubes. You know this is not how she is doing it, but each time you look away you have the impression that she is lifting the cheese and carrots with a single finger and popping them into her mouth. There are numerous embellishments to the story. You all listen, although for part of her account, the murderer and Mr. Kindt put their heads together and murmur. While she speaks, you try lifting an olive with your index finger and send it rolling toward Tulip, who doesn't notice its approach. It leaves a line of oil on the dark wood, a faint trace of its pointless trajectory. The murderer, whom you think you have just heard say "the Benny problem," although it could just as easily have been "the Lenny or the Kenny problem," pulls his head away from Mr. Kindt's, reaches over, winks at you, and plucks it up.

The buzzer sounds and the knockout's friend has arrived, only it is three friends not one. So now you are dining in company with seven people, one of whom is a murderer, or actually two of whom are murderers, you find out after you've all begun tucking into Mr. Kindt's heavy beef and carrot and shiitake stew.

I have just recently, says the second murderer, by way of introduction, become one.

Job, I say.

I go by Anthony, he says.

No one else makes any introductory statement.

Mr. Kindt, who has been seeing to something in the kitchen, comes and puts his hand on your shoulder and leans close and tells you that although it had never crossed his mind prior to your "kind intervention," he has given some desultory thought to your offer to help him.

Yeah? you say.

Tonight, my boy, he says, there might be something you could do, or that you might wish to do, and that I would be happy for you to do, if you decide to.

His hand presses into your shoulder and you notice the first murderer looking and smiling at you and you notice Tulip looking at the first murderer and smiling at him.

Does it possibly have anything to do with me murdering anyone? you say.

Yes, Mr. Kindt says. I hope the prospect doesn't bother you.

Not at all, you say, not sure how else to answer, given the hush you feel surrounding you.

That's fine, Henry, Mr. Kindt says, and returns to his seat.

Not at all, you say again.

Then the first murderer begins talking about the close connection between the sugar industry and the art world in Europe, and Mr. Kindt is all ears.

The connection is very clear, says the murderer.

I'm sure it is, says Mr. Kindt.

The knockout is talking again too—she has started up a conversation with Tulip and the two other friends. The two friends watch her very closely, their heads making small, quick gestures, and Tulip pours and sips brandy and you, although you are just slightly discomfited by the outcome of your offer to reciprocate Mr. Kindt's kindness, eat your stew.

It is as if, the murderer says, all the great works were dipped in and coated with sugar . . .

And the knockout says, and that is how, after the second incident, I repaired my arm . . .

I have been tempted, at the Munch Museum for instance, though I did not in fact do it, to slip forward, tongue-first, and test the veracity of this proposition . . .

You can see, if you look closely, that it really was very badly damaged, and that my method was quite effective . . .

Of course I know I would be disappointed . . .

In the final analysis, there was no lasting harm . . .

I find Munch most fascinating, but not for *The Scream.* I admire *The Scream,* in fact once I owned a good print, but I have never found it fascinating . . .

Look, you can still see it . . .

Etc.

Later, after dinner, you have a chance to speak privately with the knockout.

Wanna come home with me, take a number, she says.

You withdraw.

Job, who goes by Anthony, a.k.a. the second murderer, whom you have not seen at the bar in quite some time, is standing near the window. Dark hair, long, taut muscles. Very handsome.

Hey, you say.

Evening, he says.

You ask him if he minds talking.

As long as it isn't about my name or about my former place of employment or about anything personal, he says.

So how you got involved in this is out-of-bounds?

He thinks a minute. He shrugs. Tulip's a friend, he says. She told me about the opening. She introduced me around. I've got debts.

And Tulip's got a lot of friends, you say.

Anthony looks over at Tulip, who is bent over talking to the knockout. They are quite a pair. Your heart executes a perfect backflip and hits the water without a splash.

He turns back to you, one of his eyebrows raised. Next question, he says.

I'm not interviewing you.

You could have fooled the fuck out of me.

O.K., how did your first murder go?

You want me to talk about that?

Talk, you say.

He goes over to the table, takes a piece of stew-soaked bread off his plate, puts some cheese on it, and comes back.

It was fucked, he says, inserting the lion's portion of the bread into his mouth, chewing then leaning in close. He smells like lemon balm and lavender. There are one or two beads of sweat on his muscular throat. Some skin connected to his jaw twitches like someone is sticking it with a miniature cattle prod. Past his right shoulder, through the window and the black netting, the lights of Tompkins Square bob and glitter. Fucked up. Bizarre. Unpleasant. Messy. Yuck. Pick a word. I didn't like it at all. And I'll tell you something else, it wasn't even supposed to *be* a murder, it was just supposed to be a warning, a little friendly advice, cease and desist, pursue other avenues, get the fuck out of town. Just ask *them*.

"Them" is the two friends, two young women, fraternal twins, he notes, whose job, he says, during such jobs, is, when/if necessary, to hold people down. They both stand and step forward. The one with straight, shoulder-length jet-black hair grins and flexes her suddenly impressive arm muscles. The one with straight, shoulder-length pomegranate-colored hair grins, reaches back and snaps the loose material of her pants, and locks the suddenly impressive muscles in her thighs.

I'm not sure I entirely get what you're saying, you say, not quite sure who you are saying it to.

At this, Tulip steps forward, pulls her hands out of her back pockets, and says, show me how the takedown/immobilizing thing gets done.

A piece of floor is chosen, a table is pushed aside. Mr. Kindt, who has been smothering strawberries in heavy cream in the kitchen, comes in and beams. The first murderer clears his throat and crosses his arms. A silence broken only by a forlorn rattling in the wall and the muffled clanking of wind and scaffolding descends upon your company. The fraternal twins nod, then do something and in half a heartbeat Tulip is lying down very still on the carpet smiling and breathing quickly with her arms and legs pinned and a knee pressed against her chest. For effect, you suppose, the first murderer then walks forward, bends over, and gently slaps Tulip's cheek. They let her go, and you all clap, and then, as if the front door was stage right, the two friends walk out.

So now you are six for cream and strawberries and then four because the knockout is no longer feeling well, she has announced, and you have watched her, arm in arm with Anthony, walk out the door. Instead of being more than slightly discomfited, instead of thinking very actively about Anthony and his distaste for what Mr. Kindt has asked you to do, however, you stand there wishing the two friends had held *you* down, had looked coldly across your body as they bent over *you*, had pressed a knee into *your* chest, so you ask Tulip how it was and she says, quite fascinating and not too painful, and you say, show me, and she says, shhh.

The first murderer is speaking. He is looking at you.

He says, Time which antiquates Antiquities, and hath an art to make dust of all things, hath yet spared these minor Monuments. In vain we hope to be known by open and visible conservatories, when to be unknown was the means of their continuation and obscurity their protection: If they dyed by violent hands, and were thrust into their Urnes, these bones become considerable, and some old Philosophers would honour them, whose souls they conceived most pure, which were thus snatched from their bodies; and to retain a stranger propension unto them whereas they weariedly left a languishing corps, and with fain desires of re-union. If they fell by long and aged decay, yet wrapt up in the bundle of time, they fall into indistinction, and make but one blot with Infants.

While the murderer is talking, Mr. Kindt nods, and says, lovely, and closes his eyes, and you find yourself thinking of someone you once knew, and how she listened to poetry. This person, whom you once knew very well it seemed, listened with her eyes half shut and her small, dark hands curled around a drink at a table lost in the smoke of the KGB bar. You shake your head. You look at Tulip. She is tall, exquisite. Her fingers are long. You think of the knockout. You think, I should have taken a number. You stop thinking. The murderer keeps talking, and your own eyes close, and the room revolves around you, and the murderer says, If we begin to die when we live, and long life be but a prolongation of death; our life is a sad composition, and you open your eyes and the murderer is still looking at you, and you think, the composition *is* sad, it is very sad, yes, it is sad, says Mr. Kindt, from somewhere far away, and the murderer, in the most tender voice, continues speaking to you.

TEN

A polar bear can smell a rotting carcass from ten miles away. Not being a polar bear or anything else with the intuitive equivalent of an exceptional olfactory apparatus, it stands to reason that I can't. So I shouldn't feel bad. About not getting it. Right.

I know something about polar bears because once Mr. Kindt, who came often in his white slippers and light-blue gown after that first night to visit, and who proved at first to be very kind, very sweet, and more than a little amusing, watched a program on them with me. He came into my room, as he usually did, after dark, and slipped under my covers, and on the television set that hangs so firmly suspended above my bed by its mechanical arm, we watched polar bears swim and hunt and fight. We watched polar bears ride walruses, trying to kill them, hurting them terribly and being hurt terribly in return, and we watched polar bears carefully lick their tiny cubs. We watched polar bears bark impressively at Arctic foxes that came too close, and we watched them, presumably starving, wander with who knows what in their minds far out over the ice. We also watched them swimming both from above the surface of the water and from below. From below you could see the handsome reflection of the white bears on the water's surface, so that it seemed they were swimming, simultaneously, in two places—one as lovely and as ghostly as the other. We watched and watched, wishing, we agreed, that the program would never end. At one point, Mr. Kindt made some sort of a high-pitched growling sound. I did the same. Neither of us sounded remotely bearlike. We sounded more like the plump young seals that polar bears love so much to eat. We laughed a great deal at this and nudged at each other with our elbows. Mr. Kindt flipped over on all fours and cut capers on the bed. I'm a polar bear hunting its prey, he said. I laughed. He did the growl and bit my ankle through the covers. He bit so hard it made my eyes water and left marks. I didn't want to say anything to spoil our fun so I did a little writhing and groaning and laughed with him when he let go. In short, it was the sort of program we enjoyed. Nature or history. We also liked programs about economic and cultural issues, although such programs sometimes proved to be too much for Mr. Kindt. After we watched a documentary about the difficulties of the North Sea fishing industries, which largely focused on the age-old trials and tribulations of herring fishermen and the shiny little herring itself, for example, I asked Job to bring me a box of tissues to keep by my bed.

Get a fucking box of tissues yourself, Job said.

Mr. Kindt was very delicate with his tissues, dabbing carefully at his eyes and softly blowing his nose, always folding the tissue at least twice after he had used it before throwing it away. I am not sure why it appealed to me to lie or sit next to this fastidious old gentleman who was capable at one moment of biting my ankle and the next of breaking down into tears, most energetically, as it occurred, about fish, most pronouncedly when they were filmed lying on the docks in great, rotting piles. Maybe it was because he cried and blew his nose without making a sound, or because he seemed to weigh nothing as he lay there beside me, or because he was so short and awkwardly built and made his remarks in over-long sentences, or because, let's face it, he was so funny-looking, like two of those inflatable punch dolls glued together at the bottom so that instead of springing back up when they're hit they just roll around on the floor.

During his early days in the city, he told me when I asked him about his breakdown during the herring program, he had been adversely affected by a stint as a driver for a company called Fish Lines Quality Frozen Products, which had involved both loading and unloading "the endless boxes of mangled, frozen, breaded fish corpses," all of them destined for undistinguished fates on the more or less miserable shelves of second-tier outer-borough grocery stores. I giggled a little when he said the last part. He patted my hand and said that while he hadn't meant his comment to be humorous, he could understand how it might seem so. Especially when morphine was involved. In truth, he said, when he cast his mind back to those unpleasant days, the image that came to him—of his sweaty, dirty, scowling face crowned by an oversized, moldy Fish Lines delivery driver hat and of his hands completely lost in an enormous pair of vile-smelling Fish Lines insulated gloves—made him smile. When I asked him what had prompted him to take the job in the first place, he said he had accepted the position, which he had kept for far too long, (1) because Fish Lines, as everyone in those days knew, had once stood for quality and freshness in aquatic comestibles and (2) in order to put something in the purse that was growing only fitfully larger through his efforts as a thief.

What kind of things did you steal? I asked him.

Oh, this and that, he said.

Any capes? Any copper coins?

Mr. Kindt raised an eyebrow and smiled.

So you were listening to me that night.

You still haven't gotten me that reproduction.

That's very true, Henry. But at any rate, that sort of thing, capes and cows and whatnot, was much, much earlier.

All right, I said.

(3), he said, one of his personal eccentricities was a lifelong love of presenting himself in different guises. He had, and the thought now instilled in him both amusement and disgust, admired from afar the look of the Fish Lines drivers as they shepherded their frozen charges around the outer boroughs in their long-since-vanished silver trucks.

Little did I know, he said, that slipping into that uniform would turn me into such a caricature, such a clown. Or that dealing every day in frozen, rumpled boxes of mashed fish products would fill me with such horror.

I used to steal wallets at work, I said.

And? he said.

And I got caught. I'm better at it now.

I'm sure you are. He tapped my knee once or twice then pulled what looked like a cracker out of the pocket of his robe and put it into his mouth. He chewed a little, swallowed, then looked out the window.

There is some sort of netting out there, he said.

I know.

He looked back at me and shrugged.

I once stole a box of the foul product I was meant to deliver to a family restaurant called Knudsen's on Staten Island, he said. I took it home, opened it, gazed for a time at the half-thawed oily mess, tried to imagine the wads of white flesh I held in my hand back into the sleek bodies they had come from, failed, and flushed the contents down the toilet.

Back into the water, I said.

A mockery of water. Knudsen's called and I was asked to leave Fish Lines the next day. I sent the president of the company a letter reminding him that Fish Lines had once dealt only in the freshest of fish and scolding him for trucking in such shoddy, indeed degrading, merchandise. He wrote me back that he was a businessman and that business was good and that I was just "a bowl of sour soup some old lady stuck her foot in," end of story. Imagine! And, yes, go ahead and laugh.

Mr. Kindt's other eccentricities included a love of country-and-western music. In particular, he liked what he called "the darkly crackling voice of Hank Williams and the gravelly ballads of Johnny Cash." Often, when he came to visit me, he would bring a little tape deck along with him. If there was nothing we cared to watch on TV, he would set the tape deck by my bed and we would listen. Sometimes, when I wasn't feeling too well, he would leave the tape deck behind, and it is true that listening to Johnny Cash singing through the rags and dust and years in his throat about falling into rings of fire and Hank Williams telling stories about steam engines and lonely miles of track was somehow comforting.

Well, maybe not comforting. Or anyway not *always* comforting. Recently when Mr. Kindt has lent me his tape deck, there has been precious little comfort in these tapes for me. One Hank Williams song in particular makes for difficult listening. In it, he asks if you think that when your time comes you will be ready to go, and if you think that once you are dead and are under the cold clay you will be satisfied with what you have done and who you have been. And, such unpleasant questions aside, he calls shadows "shadders," and the "shadders" creep, and if you sit there listening to the song alone, which is what I've been doing these last few nights, even right this second, and there are strange lights flashing around you, there are bars on the windows and strangers passing in the corridors, there are wires, a rotting carcass you couldn't smell before it really started to stink, an oily box filled with mashed fish, you are thinking too much, you always think too much, if all that, well then, basically, shit.

ELEVEN

Let's take a walk, kid, says the murderer whose name, he tells me as we're leaving Mr. Kindt's building, is Cornelius.

Nice to meet you, Cornelius, I say.

Yeah, sure, kid, sure, this way.

"This way" is up Avenue B for a while, past the curving lanes of the park, past the restaurants and shops and brightly lit tenements, past Tenth and Eleventh, with their relatively quaint buildings and spindly trees, then over to Avenue A. Cornelius walks fast. Cornelius is dressed a little shabbily, and he's a little hunched over and fat. On some nights in the East Village everyone is fat. We passed this fat guy. We passed this fat gal. We passed a pickle shop window and I caught a piece of our reflection and, yes, no question, I'm a little fat too.

I was fatter than the average as a kid. My aunt, who was a very nice woman, my God, she was nice—especially when she would smack me with the spoon—used to refer to me as *husky*. Boy, you're husky, she would say. Then she would smack me. I later gathered that she had gotten hold of *husky* from a TV commercial for young boys' jeans. Young boys with slow metabolisms, who had indulged too frequently on Big Macs and double cheeseburgers and Twinkies and Mars Bars and large vanilla Tyrols were husky. To tell the truth, *husky*'s probably not a bad way to describe me now.

So there we are, husky Henry and fat Cornelius walking up Avenue A, past the local denizens, with their somber eye shadow and faux fur and polyester pants and nonprescription nerd glasses and cell phones and gas masks.

Where are we going, Mr. Murderer? I say.

Nowhere, shut up, Henry, we're here, don't be a motormouth, he says.

A motormouth? I say.

He turns into a doorway next to an unlit faded dry cleaner's, buzzes, tells me to wait, and goes in.

A couple of cabs hum by, then a Mustang painted up to look like the Mexican flag and a cyclist wearing a black helmet and goggles and dark-green socks. It takes me a second to realize that this cyclist is my old friend Fish. I don't call out to him. He probably wouldn't stop anyway. I owed him money for too long and obliged him to bang on my door until I came out and, in lieu of payment, let him stagger off with my TV. Fish used to work as a copy editor at a short-lived golf magazine based in midtown. We both lost our jobs around the same time, both slid around the same time, the difference being that Fish slid voluntarily and now lives, by choice, in an unusual squat situation and rides around the East Village in his goggles.

I do a little near-silent whistling. I register that I'm whistling ABBA's "Take a Chance on Me" and stop. I don't really, I think, want anyone to do any such thing. An old man in one of those colorless zip-up jackets and a beat-up porkpie takes a long time to walk by me. I nod at him. He does not look at me, does not, in fact, seem to see me. A dollop of street light falls onto his face. I can smell lentils, saffron, burnt plastic. My mind follows him home, where I imagine him unlocking a door, pulling it open, stepping in, clearing his throat, and calling out an unreciprocated greeting into the darkness. Time is not our friend, I think. I start whistling again. ABBA again. After about five minutes, Cornelius is back.

All right, good to go, he says, handing me a key.

Good to go in what way exactly?

You'll see, just get up there, it's on the fourth floor.

I look at him.

He frowns at me.

You're Mr. Kindt's buddy, right?

Right.

So why are we still standing here talking?

He wants me to do this? This specifically?

Let's just say he thought you might *enjoy* doing, yes, this.

O.K., but enjoy doing what? I'm supposed to go up there and murder someone?

Apartment 4A, lock sticks a little, you got gloves? Put them on and go the fuck up.

It was one of those East Village buildings that hadn't been fixed up and would likely see a wrecking ball before long. The stairwell was steep and dirty and narrow and badly lit and poorly painted and there were deep cracks at the base of its walls. High-pitched, unhappy sounds came out of a couple of the graffiti-covered doors. As Cornelius had said, the lock did stick but not too badly. I took a deep breath, bit down on my tongue, exhaled, and went in. And while in the wake of my conversation with Anthony I was expecting to come face-to-face with something strange, possibly exciting, more probably unpleasant, it certainly wasn't *that*. *That* was the knockout, who was apparently, literally, knocked out. Lying on the kitchen linoleum wearing nothing but a sign on her stomach that read, when I got close enough to kind-of inspect her and read it, KILL ME.

Yeah right, hah, hah, KILL ME, I thought.

But just then a door opened and the fraternal twins from dinner came out. I can't even describe what it was they were doing and how it was they were moving. Maybe you've seen contortionists in action before. Or at least photos thereof. Basically, something is seriously wrong with their spines. And with other things: their sockets, their primary joints and articulations. They had shucked the loose-fitting gear they had been wearing at Mr. Kindt's in favor of pale-blue sequined leotards. They made circles around the room—hideous, freaky, fascinating circles—each time stepping over the knockout lying on the linoleum. Once one of them misstepped, or, maybe, didn't misstep, and joggled one of the knockout's patently artificial, definitely torpedo-class breasts. Then they rushed me and before I could move I had two grimy feet in my face. Each of the feet was holding a piece of folded paper pinched between the first and second toes. I took one of them, then the other, then the feet went away and the two of them went back to doing their contorted dance around the room. All of this was happening in your basic, crappy, old-school East Village kitchen. There was one long window with the inevitable bars and a couple of bedraggled sun-starved plants. Blech paint job, birdcage with a stuffed parrot in it, some oil-grimed hot-pepper Christmas lights, a sink out of something by Hieronymus Bosch, a view of an air shaft, and all the standard low-budget, largely defective kitchen implements. I unfolded the first piece of paper. It read, "In the drawer next to the stove." I unfolded the second piece. It read, "Get the knife."

I should probably clarify, if it means anything, that on this occasion at least, Cornelius, the murderer, wasn't really all that much like I have most lately described him. He was more like I described him at dinner—sort of distant and mysterious, given to pronouncing what Mr. Kindt later described as the "sonorous conundrums" of seventeenth-century surgeon-philosophers. He certainly wasn't overweight. Just like I'm not. He was, if not emaciated, then quite slender, and he wore, with his own floppy black hat, an elegant black hunting cape, and we walked a good deal farther before arriving at our destination than I made it sound like above, and we talked.

How do you know Mr. Kindt? I asked him.

Isn't he wonderful? the murderer said.

Yes, he's my dear friend now, I said. How do you know him?

We are old colleagues.

Colleagues?

Yes, in fact, it was Aris who set me out on my current path. And I him on his.

I see.

Yes.

Are you from upstate?

Near Cooperstown.

Did you see him swim the lake?

I lost money on it. Lots and lots of money. More money than I like to think of, even now.

I'm sorry to hear that.

We were young. There was drink involved. I miscalculated.

Mr. Kindt helped you to get started on murdering?

Indeed.

How so?

He both gave me the idea and helped with its early implementation.

And you've been successful?

Terrifically.

No shortage of work?

None.

Pays well?

Very fairly. Even with the sliding scale we have recently implemented. There is a real need, it would seem, a deep-seated impulse following the horror downtown. An impulse that manifests as desire.

Desire?

We offer the modalities to perform an act of ritual negation. One is able, on one's own terms, to say no.

I told him it sounded like he was talking about suicide.

Ah, but there is external agency. Underscored by the transaction, the exchange of cash.

Euthanasia then.

Well, that would certainly be closer. Be we are not discussing in this instance individuals in their apparent final extremities. And we are discussing symbols.

How exactly did Mr. Kindt help you?

He was the first victim. The first beneficiary, albeit of a primitive version of the system.

I don't follow you.

Ah, but someday perhaps—he had reached the door and buzzed—you will.

I stood alone on the street for a few minutes. External agency, I thought. Primitive version. The air smelled of lentils and saffron. My friend Fish rode by.

Incidentally, I like hunting capes. In fact, I decided I would like to have one. I told Mr. Kindt the next day how much I liked them, and he told me that he, too, liked hunting capes very much and that the namesake of his namesake had, in fact, once attempted to steal one from someone and had paid quite heavily.

You have two namesakes?

Don't we all?

Maybe technically. If you're a king or something.

Mr. Kindt said he liked this idea of kings and went on about it for some time. When he was done, I asked him how heavily the namesake of his namesake, or whatever, had paid.

Think of lead and other troublingly dense elements and how authoritatively, once released, they fall, Mr. Kindt said, laughing, and adding a "dear young man," and the conversation ended there, except that one of the next times I went over to Mr. Kindt's he had a hunting cape to give me. Just like Cornelius's. That's the kind of friend he was. Anything, he loved to say, for a friend.

Or for a fish, I once joked as we sat late one night over brandy.

They like oxygen, Mr. Kindt, who was quite drunk, said, but of course are not fond of air. Still. They are like.

But more graceful. Absolute and graceful. Imagine great silver flocks. Underwater birds with sharp, powerful wings.

I had a dream about fish once during this period. In it, I was both fish and viewer of fish, and Mr. Kindt was a fish too. He swam up to me and said, you are not just any sort of fish, my dear boy, you are a herring. Then I was a herring on a laboratory table. The experiment was to see why it was that herring might die immediately upon leaving the water, a characteristic that, though long and widely believed to afflict them, was never proved. Tulip—and this gave the dream a vaguely visionary quality—was presiding. She had a scalpel and was describing and making incisions. I could simultaneously see up into the room and down into the laboratory table. The interior of the table was shot through with dark red veins and shafts of blue minerals. Mr. Kindt was in there. He was a fish, probably like me a herring, in a black hat and hunting cape. I understood, in the way you do in dreams, that he was hiding. From Tulip. From all of us. He was trying to make one of his fins stretch up to his mouth so that he could indicate to me that I should shut up.

I did. To no avail. Suddenly he was lying on the laboratory table, and Tulip was working on him and, like in the Rembrandt print he had up on his wall, people had gathered around. There was the murderer and there was Anthony, only in the dream he was Job again, and there was someone you don't know because I haven't mentioned him and there was the knockout, with a jagged red line around her neck. She was fully clothed in the dream. She was smiling and was very interested in the proceedings, as we all were, including Mr. Kindt. He was trying to look at what Tulip was doing but couldn't, because he had something very wrong with his neck. I therefore took it upon myself to describe to him what was going on.

Tulip, I told him, has now opened up your arm and is explaining to the audience, with the help of a diagram in an anatomy book, everything there is to know about it. Your arm is both hideous and beautiful, now that its interior is being seen, considered, set into categories, accorded its right and proper context. Tulip is not looking at you any longer. She is looking at the audience. The audience is looking at the anatomy book. She has produced some kind of a clamp and is holding up your hand. Falsification, Tulip now says, sits at the center of everything.

Just as it did in the awful East Village kitchen, with its cracked, moldy baseboards, its smell of rancid lard and, possibly, leaking gas. The knockout was on the floor, supposedly unconscious. The two friends were moving like enormous crabs around me. Before long, they began to blur into bands of pale light. I stood there, hardly even breathing, for what seemed like ages, as if time, the part of it that corresponded to me, had stopped or slowed way down, while the part of it that corresponded to the rest of the room, including the contortionists and the knockout, had sped up, like in that episode of the original *Star Trek* where some crew members appear to be frozen and others are moving too quickly to be seen. Anyway, this strange, messy movement I had trouble fully grasping was happening around me and there I stood like a scorpion stuck in Lucite. Then time, the real murderer, started up again, and I could clearly see them and didn't like what I saw, and I felt obliged to do something, so I said, good-bye, knockout! Good-bye, contortionists! Fuck all of you! I walked out the door, went back downstairs, and punched elegant or inelegant Cornelius in the mouth.

No, I didn't. Of course I didn't. What I did was turn and lock the door behind me, pull my gloves on tighter, then say, so you want me to open the kitchen drawer and get out the knife?

TWELVE

Mr. Kindt loved a good cigar, and he would always, with impeccable courtesy, offer me one. Dutch Masters was the brand he preferred, and he didn't mind if I chuckled about it like it was a joke. In fact, as we have seen, not only did he like for me to laugh about things, he insisted I do so. You have such a very pleasant laugh, it's so rich and hearty, I find it invigorating, he would say. He was just about as quick with a compliment as he was with a cigar. Apparently I had nice manners and nice features and "fine, strong shoulders" and a nice way of holding a plastic-tipped Premium. Generally, if I was smoking alone, I smoked Merits, but in Mr. Kindt's company it was cigars. Mr. Kindt thought very little indeed of cigarettes, "those miniature albino cigars," "those blatant disease-carrying delivery systems for brand names." There was no reason whatsoever, he said, to suck smoke all the way down into the lungs, which was the custom with cigarettes. The mouth, which held the tongue and the mechanisms of taste, was the appropriate receptacle. Its highly permeable membranes eagerly invited tobacco's active compounds to enter the "inward-leading complex" of blood vessels they played host to. And of course, he added, cigars tasted much better. I wasn't at all sure about this last point, especially when it came to Dutch Masters, but I didn't argue. I didn't argue either when Mr. Kindt would talk, with a funny little smile on his lips, about how pleasant it would be to die, if one had to, by having one's throat annihilated by cancer, or lungs filled with fragrant tar. When one is in the early, enthusiastic throes of a friendship, one lets a great deal slide.

Out in the hospital's so-called garden, the air was either too warm or too cold, depending, often, on how we were feeling and, in my case, how recently I had been given meds. Always there were the sirens coming or going and the sound of sledgehammers and saws and earthmovers in the distance where they were removing rubble. Consequently, it was only in the late evening that you could hear birds or the occasional windblown tree. The temperature or noise level notwithstanding, there from time to time we would sit on one of the low concrete benches and puff and watch the sickly pigeons and Mr. Kindt would grin with his bad teeth, rub his forehead, and discourse. It was during one of these speeches that I learned that the herring population in the North Sea had more than once become quite devastated due to overfishing, and that one clear day many years before his misadventures with Fish Lines, before we had watched our program together, when he had read about this devastation over a cup of coffee in his favorite Amsterdam haunt, he had burst into tears.

Sadness builds like sediment with the kind of predictability that still manages to astonish, the kind that often ends by masking its original cause, he said. Years before that cup of coffee, I stood heartbroken in front of a fishmonger's and watched his knife, guided as much by physical memory as by his blinking green eyes ringed with flecks of blood, destroy the animate integrity of his dead or merely dying charges.

But you like to eat fish, I said. I haven't seen you cry when you do that.

Oh, I love to eat fish, of course, herring in particular. It is practically a sickness with me. It is perhaps because of this love, which I have had since childhood, that the whole question became so acute. You know the old adage, my boy: touch one part of the web and the whole thing quivers. I can clearly remember as a boy biting the stomach out of a tiny pickled sardine and thinking, but something large and awful will soon do the same to me. Most of us get over these little waking nightmares, but not I. At least not that one.

It was in the garden, likewise, that I learned how to say "you fucking ball-bag" in Dutch, along with other little bits of terminology. It was pretty pleasant, really. When he wasn't discoursing, Mr. Kindt was endlessly curious about me, and I found myself saying all sorts of things. I talked about my time on the street under the scaffolding on Great Jones and about my two cats that had become one and then none. A lot of what I talked about, of course, was Dr. Tulp. About the short row of silver pens she kept in her breast pocket. And about how her long cold fingers, in the process of going about their ministrations, would occasionally, I imagined, make unexplained movements across my chest. These movements would, later, when the ward had gone quiet and she had returned for a follow-up "consultation," occasionally be accomplished with the help of one of her pens. The pen she would use would be dry but the marks it left would be wet. She would dig with her pen until there were neat rows of red trenches then she would lean very close and clean me up with large alcohol-soaked swabs.

I don't know why I imagine that last part, I told Mr. Kindt.

I'm sure I don't either, Henry, Mr. Kindt said. But we all have our little fantasies, our little gropings in the dark. Who knows what we find there? Who can say? I have groped in the dark and found my fingers around people's throats and theirs, in turn, around mine. Who knows where it all leads?

Also, I would tell him about my girlfriend, Carine. And about the French poets she loved so much and about her handsome vintage clothing.

Carine was nothing like Dr. Tulp. For one thing she was not tall, for another she was French-*ish*. I once asked her about this "ish" thing when I was feeling grouchy, and she said she was French by descent and that she had studied French language and literature in school and had lived in France and was a Francophile and was completely and legitimately French-identified. I said that seemed a little stretched and a tad fake, and she, quite legitimately, kicked me hard under the table with her pointy vintage shoe.

I did not study French in school. I did not study much at all in school. A few classics, a little mimicry, a little attitude, that's about it. This was a sore point, at times, in our relationship.

No, I have not read that, I would say.

Well, do you want to read it? she would say.

I'm not sure, I don't know what it's about, I would say.

I just got done telling you, *mon amour,* I've been telling you about it for the past twenty minutes, she would say.

Can you recap? I would say.

No, she would say.

Please, I would say.

It's about disgust and misogyny and the sexual ramifications of the 1968 student uprisings in France and the current impotence of the contemporary French novel, she would say.

You're just bragging, I would say.

And she would say, you're cute, but don't be a dickhead.

I would like to note again that during our sessions and when she came to see me in the ward, I became very fond of Dr. Tulp. I even took to affecting, both in Dr. Tulp's presence and out of it, a slight Dutch accent. Even though Dr. Tulp, who had been in the States for some time, did not really have one. Actually, Dr. Tulp's accent was Boston if it was anything. It wasn't Boston enough to be comical, if Boston makes you, as it does me, laugh to hear in quantity; but there was something there that made you, when you heard it, think of lips being pulled back to expose a lot of white teeth. I have already mentioned my fantasy about Dr. Tulp carving my chest with her pen so I might as well note that there were moments when it occurred to me to imagine waking up one night with Dr. Tulp's white teeth sunk deeply but not uncomfortably into my throat. I haven't told you about my teeth yet. For now, let's just say they could use a little servicing. As could, as I have said, Mr. Kindt's. Mr. Kindt wasn't big on the oral hygiene. Frankly, he was not big on much hygiene at all, but he did love a hot shower. Every day he would have one. I don't say any soap was involved in the shower, or, rather, that I can confirm that there was soap involved, but it was hot. Once or twice when I was visiting him in his room, he asked me to hand him a towel. Once, he asked me to hand him a towel then sit down outside the shower. When I asked him why he wanted me to do this, he said he just wanted, at that moment, to know that I was near.

I have not felt, he said, entirely myself today. Or rather it would perhaps be more accurate to say that today I have felt too much like myself, that my carefully acquired external layers have sloughed off, leaving my interior exposed.

What does it feel like? I asked.

Not at all good.

Not at all good how?

Quite terrible, you know.

You mean like the big thing eating you.

Well, yes. But also it is as if I had retracted, horribly, as if everything around me had begun to blur.

I didn't say anything.

It has happened before. It can make me scream.

He was standing, a small yellow form behind the semi-transparent shower curtain.

Do you feel like screaming now? I said.

It is never a question of feeling like it, he said. I just scream.

In the meantime though, Mr. Kindt did not scream—he cried and breathed too heavily and said odd, occasionally corny things—and life in the hospital continued much as it had. I met twice a week with Dr. Tulp, who did not sink her teeth into my throat or carve my chest with her pen, but instead asked me questions about patterns of redundancy and potential or actual seams of discontent within, and the location of, my family, and I received nightly and sometimes daily meds and continued to steal items that I passed on to Job. I also read books suggested by Mr. Kindt, like part of a fat history of the Dutch East India company—basically a chronicle of brilliant greed and unvarnished corruption—which he left on my night table one morning, magazines that Job brought in for me, and things I put my hands on as I made my way around the hospital. Nothing I read though seemed as interesting as *The Rings of Saturn,* and I often pulled it out of my drawer and flipped through it. After I had read a page or two, I would lie back on my bed or go and lie down if I hadn't been lying down already and look up at the ceiling and think vague, melodramatic, mostly borrowed thoughts about playing some key part in the Taiping Rebellion in China or helping to end the early-twentieth-century Congolese rubber trade or carrying on a doomed but sort of elegant love affair with the daughter of a vicar. If I was dozy, which I often was, these rarefied thoughts would shift ground, so that before long, instead of carrying the banner for the failing Chinese rebels or riding across the heath to deliver a bundle of roses under cover of dark, or landing at night to join the Irish separatists, I would be patrolling the ramparts of some besieged fortress culled from the fantasy novels of my childhood, brandishing an unbreakable blade, setting my jaw, and waiting for some hideous onslaught. Well, that's stupid, but the reason I bring it up is that one afternoon just as the huge black arrows had begun to fly, just as the screams and battle cries had begun to take over my skull, I opened my eyes and—in one of the developments that has slowly helped lead me to a better, though still imperfect, understanding of my position here— found myself looking at my aunt.

THIRTEEN

The morning after my first murder, Mr. Mancini, the manager of The Fidelity, where I had been staying since I left the hospital, knocked on my door and told me I had a phone call.

Who is it? I said.

Yeah, yeah, let me check with my secretary, shitface, he said, smiling.

Since my arrival at his establishment, Mr. Mancini had called me shitface six times that I knew of, and once when I asked him if I could have an extra key to my room he had taken a baseball bat out from under his desk and smacked it against the wall. He also smiled constantly and really unpleasantly, and, even though I wanted to try very badly, he was too big to even imagine beating the shit out of.

Actually, I had imagined beating the shit out of him several times. Each time, as I threw the last, devastating punch, aiming for his throat after I had worked over his midsection and face, I thought of previous imagined triumphs and said, who's the shitface now?

Anyway, after I had put some clothes on, I went down to the lobby, attempted to ignore Mr. Mancini, who had taken up position behind his desk, and picked up the greasy yellow phone that sat on a stack of old coin-collector magazines in the corner. Then I walked over to the

Odessa Café on Tompkins Square and took a seat at the back and waited for the knockout to walk in.

It's not every day that you have the opportunity to break bread with someone you've murdered the night before, and while it had all been, to borrow and permute Anthony's vocabulary, unpleasantly messy (basically I had fucked it up), continuing the acquaintance appealed greatly to me, not least because as I left, one of the contortionists had stuck two hundred dollars in my pocket with her foot.

I had spent a good quarter of my earnings at the Horseshoe, drinking Cape Cods and hoping that, even though he didn't work there anymore, Anthony would show up so that we could compare notes. He did not. I finally asked the bartender on duty about him and was told that Job, if that's who I meant, hadn't been there for weeks.

The knockout and all her nice proportions arrived a few minutes after I did. She was wearing a maroon slip, a black leather bomber, pink-tinted glasses, and a kiss-my-ass grin that she tore off and tossed in my lap as she sat down.

Hi, I said.

Get us some drinks, and soup, I want borscht, she said.

A waitress who had clearly been eating too many pierogi for too many years and who was wearing a lot of eye makeup and what looked to me like a wig she had possibly inherited from a great-aunt in the old country came over and called me sweetheart and I ordered.

While we waited, the knockout pulled out a cell phone and made a couple of calls, one to a guy named Bob, who apparently did bodywork for her, and one to Mr. Kindt.

He wants to talk to you, she said.

About what?

She didn't bother to answer, just handed me the phone then got up and went in the direction of the toilets.

Henry? Mr. Kindt said.

Yes, I said.

Come to see me this afternoon, dear boy, after you have finished with your lunch and conversation.

I killed this lunch partner of mine last night, you know, *murdered* her, I said.

Yes, well, that is what she wants to talk to you about—listen to her, she is quite articulate and quite direct. She can be of great help.

Great help with what?

Mr. Kindt laughed. With any, if you should choose to carry them out, future murders, he said.

I knew what you meant.

I know you did. Was the pay satisfactory?

It was.

Good, and there will of course be more. So for now just think of last night as a test, a trial run. A little fine-tuning is in order, that's all.

Does Cornelius know about this lunch I'm having? I asked.

Of course he does, my boy, he is in charge, how could he not? Now, finish up there, then come and see me.

I hung up just as the borscht arrived. A couple minutes later we were both eating sweet, airy challa bread, spooning up the red stuff, drinking Cape Cods, and looking at each other.

Yeah, I know you saw me naked, so what? she said.

She leaned forward, expressing some serious décolletage,

and stuck one of her nails a little farther than was comfortable into my forearm.

Did you appreciate? she asked.

Yes, I appreciated.

Of course you did.

I had liked the afterimage so much in fact that after I had left the scene of the crime I went back to my little room in Mr. Mancini's flop and wrestled around with it for a while. But of course I didn't tell her that. Instead, I took a sip of my Cape Cod, or whatever we were drinking, probably just Coke, it doesn't matter, and said, O.K., talk to me, tell me why I'm here, tell me what I did wrong.

Everything, genius.

That's a lot.

You have a way with words.

So I'm told.

By who?

Who or whom?

Let's say who.

Let's drop it.

You talk tough, I think I like it.

Now it's you who likes something.

Who says I just started?

I looked at her. I wished we'd just said all of the preceding, even if it sounded like bad noir dialogue. I wished, after she'd said, everything, genius, and I'd said, that's a lot, that she hadn't proceeded to tell me, in detail and pretty directly, how much I sucked.

I already told Cornelius you're useless.

So what did he say?

He said I should meet with you and, if at all possible, straighten your sorry ass out.

He said it like that?

More or less.

Can you straighten my sorry ass out?

Of course I can.

Why? I mean, why bother? It's not like I asked to do this.

Why do you think?

I took a bite of borscht-soaked challa and pretended to think about it.

But why does he want me to do this? I said.

You'll have to ask him that.

I did—later, when I went over to his house.

We'll discuss motivation another day, he said. Or perhaps I should say the motivation will become clear or clearer later. In the meantime, I will just ask you, as my friend, to help me and my partner, Cornelius, in facilitating this venture. Since my earliest days as a businessman I have been interested in unusual, even improbable, transactions. Don't forget, after all, that I made my real start in affairs by swimming the length of a lake with my arms bound tightly behind me.

You didn't mention your arms being tied before.

Well they weren't, that would have been impossible. I said it just now for effect. But it was nevertheless a transforming experience. When the adventure ended I walked away from Lake Otsego a changed man.

Cornelius told me he was there.

Did he? It's true that I have known Cornelius for a very long time. He wasn't much more than a boy then. Nor, for that matter, was I. But at any rate, dear Henry, there is so very much demand for this service, and I am so grateful that you are willing to help and even indulge me.

I was. And had. I mean, the whole time I just sat there and let the knockout disparage me. Of course that hadn't been entirely about making Mr. Kindt happy. Being insulted then instructed by a beautiful woman about the subject of murder, even fake murder, while eating borscht and drinking Cape Cods or Coke counts as positive in my book.

All right, I said.

All right, what?

I mean all right, I'm enjoying this.

Good, but let's hope you're understanding it too.

If you're going to be sloppy, be sloppy in a big, big way, I said. But it's better to be neat.

She nodded.

Anthony had his problems, things got out of control, but at least he was neat, I said.

That's right.

I'm a neat thief, I said.

Even if you are, which I doubt, a neat thief and a neat murderer are not the same thing.

How so?

Degree. Other things too but mainly degree. Death is a different degree. Murder is death amplified and pinpointed. Big focused death. Big but not sloppy. What else?

It has to hurt, I said. Pain implies the actual. There has to be an implication of the actual to engender fear. Fear and the frisson that heralds it are ultimately why the checks get signed. That's why it's a good idea to knock them out, chloroform them or something.

Good.

Who writes the scripts?

It depends—sometimes the victim, sometimes Cornelius, sometimes me or the others.

What's up with those others anyway?

She didn't answer. Instead she pulled out a gun, placed it against my forehead, and pulled the trigger.

This is a story about murder—Mr. Kindt's, several other people's, my own. My own just about blew my eardrums out, scared the shit out of me, and stained my shirt paint-pellet red. The sound was so loud it slammed me back into my seat, and I just watched her as she stood, dropped a note in my lap, and, still holding the gun, which she lifted, menacingly, as if the other chambers had real bullets in them, when the waitress and one of the customers started moving toward her, walked out the door. It was only after I had wiped some of the fake blood off my face and, assuring the waitress and manager that I was all right and that, no, I wasn't going to wait to talk to the police, left myself, that I opened up the note. It read, "Round two is tonight at three o'clock," and gave an address on St. Mark's Place.

FOURTEEN

It was so strange to see my aunt sitting beside my bed, her great fat face simultaneously beaming and anxious, that I sat up, swung my bare legs over the side of the bed, and clapped her on the arm. This felt so good that I leaned forward and clapped her on the side of the head.

Go and tell them I need a shot, tell them that, then we can talk, I said.

My aunt shook her fat head, stood, walked a little way toward the door, looked back at me, and said, you're a schmuck, Henry boy, you always were, and was gone.

A minute later she was back. She came at me so fast all I had time to do was start to raise my arm before she had slapped me, good and hard like the old days, across my face.

Jesus, Aunt Lulu, I said.

I'll give you a shot, boy, you little schmuck, she said.

She raised her hand like she was going to slap me again but instead sat down, and after a couple of seconds the beaming, anxious look was back on her face.

Where you been, Henry? You left me, she said.

I shrugged.

I been worried, Henry.

I didn't say anything.

So now you live in boxes on the street. Now you do

bad, bad things and you hit your aunt when she isn't looking out for it.

I'm sorry, Aunt Lulu.

Yeah, you better be sorry, Henry. I'm your aunt. I'm
your Goddamn aunt, and I raised you, Henry. You're the
one who put an end to that. You're the one with the special way of saying thank you. Don't forget it.

I am sorry, I said.

She reached out one of her big fat hands and touched
my knee with it. I suppressed a shudder.

I'm sorry too, boy, she said.

Why did you come, Aunt Lulu? I said.

She pulled her hand back and, though her eyes were
still shining, frowned.

You know anything about these buildings falling down?

They didn't just fall, Aunt Lulu.

She smiled. Extremely brightly.

Call me Mother, like you used to when you were little,
she said.

I didn't answer. I thought of her sitting slumped at the
kitchen table, barely moving, that last time, her long, greasy
hair covering her face. I thought of her in her dirty blue
housedress feeding the cats, kicking the cats, washing the
cats. Then I thought about buildings, buildings all over the
city, falling down.

The hospital called you, Aunt Lulu? I said.

I told them I'm not paying a cent for any of this. I'm
not paying a damn red nickel for you to live in a box and
piss on the street and do bad things to people. I got nothing to do with it.

They can't make you pay anything, Aunt Lulu.

I'm not, boy. Believe me. I've got bills.

We sat there. My aunt's big fat face was beet red and she was breathing hard and I thought she might lean forward and slap me again, maybe pull the old spoon out of her bag and apply it medicinally to my skin, but somehow she was still beaming, like a smiling virus had infected her face.

I heard from that girl, she said.

What girl?

You tell her not to call me. Not ever. I got nothing to say to such as her. She was too fancy for you, Henry boy. The whole world you fell out of was too fancy.

Wait, who called you?

Aunt Lulu didn't answer. Instead she smiled hard, winked at me, and began mumbling. As she was mumbling, Mr. Kindt poked his head in the door and gestured for me to come over. I pointed at Aunt Lulu. He threw his shoulders back, dropped his head, and began moving his lips and prancing around. I slipped out of bed. Mr. Kindt was waiting for me in the hallway.

My aunt, I said.

Ah, said Mr. Kindt. Well, I'm very sorry to interrupt. I just stopped by to see if you were interested in having a smoke. I was just sitting in my room remembering my Plato and thinking about justice and right conduct and so forth. I thought you might be interested in discussing it.

Well, any other time, I said, pointing back into my room, where Aunt Lulu was still sitting by the bed, still mumbling.

Of course, said Mr. Kindt. I suspect you are very happy to see her. What is her name?

Lulu.

That's interesting.

I raised my eyebrows, flared my lips a little, and started back into the room.

One just wonders where all the wreckage gets piled, he said, where the dump trucks of history, as it were, unload the corpses they have accumulated, that they will keep accumulating. Right conduct or wrong, when a just or unjust man helps a friend or harms an enemy, the end result, if it is in any way remarkable, ends up in the dump truck. Everything else gets ground under the wheels.

That's a little grim, I said, pausing at the door.

Oh, but it is grim, Henry, Mr. Kindt said. It's very grim.

I squeezed Mr. Kindt's arm, smiled apologetically, and went back into the room. I managed to slip back into my bed without disturbing Aunt Lulu. It was strange to see her sitting there, strange and somehow reassuring. It was part of our curious fate, Mr. Kindt had said to me that very afternoon, that we should so readily keep company with our most resilient horrors.

As I thought about this and looked at her, a familiar image came to mind, of Aunt Lulu and a friend playing pinochle. It was the week of Halloween and I was sitting on the little rocker in the corner looking at them through the poorly cut rubber eyeholes of a Creature from the Black Lagoon mask. My face stung. It was also hot. Every now and then I would growl and lift my arms. They both had on smeared costume makeup. Neither of them spoke. Earlier they had sent me out into the backyard with a trowel to "dig for the devil." A cracked Coke bottle lay dripping in the middle of the floor where my father had thrown it. Before he left, for good as it turned out, he had come out to the backyard, taken the trowel from me, and told me first that he was going to go try to find my mother and second about a soda shop in the Bronx where ice-cold Coke ran nonstop out of a spigot attached to the wall.

I yawned, leaned back against my pillows, looked at the clock: Job wouldn't be back for a while. Aunt Lulu was still mumbling. She had once attended a church that encouraged its members to speak in tongues. She had not forced me to attend, but she had tried to teach me the proper technique. I went around the house after her lesson talking with my tongue sticking out. When I spoke in tongues to her, she pinched my ear and told me it wasn't something that was supposed to be done casually. Mumbling was fine though. There was a good deal of it around our household. Aunt Lulu liked to mumble to her cats. She also liked to sit in the kitchen, slightly hunched forward, and mumble to herself. Like she was doing now. Like she had been doing that day when I had stood in the doorway and, well aware that she had poured enough vodka and orange juice down her throat onto the palmful of Halcion she swallowed every day to take out a small stegosaurus, watched her head droop slowly downward toward her plate of macaroni and cheese.

After a while she took a deep breath, put her hands on her knees, and looked up.

They tell me you're in trouble, boy.

It's not that bad, Aunt Lulu.

That's a lie, boy.

I'm not lying to you, Aunt Lulu. They're doctors—they exaggerate. I'm getting good help. I've got friends here. It's under control.

I watched her take this in, turn it around once or twice, then forget it.

I'm leaving now, boy. I just came to tell you I'm not paying for you to live like a dog and do more bad things and lie in a hospital bed reading books.

Good-bye, Aunt Lulu, I said.

Good-bye, boy, she said. She smacked me again, not so hard this time. Then stood and walked out.

FIFTEEN

My ears still ringing, I put the note in my pocket and walked across the park to Mr. Kindt's. On my way, I stopped to watch some kids slugging it out over access to an open swing. It was a pretty good fight, as far as fights involving small kids go—there were actually some punches thrown and a couple of kicks—and I was a little sorry when a tall woman with a large mouth and hands the size of coffee cakes came over and broke it up. For a second it occurred to me to say something to her, to tell her to relax a little, let the kids fight, a swing, for God's sake, was worth fighting about, but then I realized I was about to pass out. I went over to a bench and sat very still, then leaned over and put my head between my knees, then, when I felt a little better, sat up and sneezed.

You've got blood all over your face and shirt, said a green-haired, well-pierced woman walking by with a three-legged wrinkle-faced dog.

I know, I just got murdered, I said.

She looked at me, the golden hoop in her right eyebrow rising significantly.

What's your dog's name? I said.

He doesn't have a name.

Does he bite?

Yes, he probably does.

Look, I'm in an interesting line of work. If I had a business card, I'd give you one, I said.

Yes, she said. I bet you would.

Can I have your number?

No.

Out of the corner of my eye I could see a woman and a young girl tilting and gently shaking what I realized was a kind of trap when I saw two mice fall out of it onto the soft dirt next to an evergreen.

What you see in this city, I said.

Every day, the woman with the three-legged dog said.

Then I left the park and went to Mr. Kindt's.

Oh, let's get you cleaned up, he said.

When we were out of the bathroom and sitting over cups of Lapsang souchong in the living room, he asked me how the meeting had gone. I said it had gone well. My head felt like someone had started a lobotomy on it, and I felt like throwing up, but otherwise it had been very pleasant and extremely informative.

I don't know her terribly well myself, but Cornelius recommends her highly, Mr. Kindt said.

I can see why he does.

I've had the privilege of seeing her at her work. She's very good. She is able to lull her victims into acquiescence merely, it seems, by speaking to them.

She's bald, I said.

I watched the corners of Mr. Kindt's mouth rise then fall, but just slightly. We sipped at our tea. Mr. Kindt asked me if, in light of the meeting, that is, he said, in light of being insulted by a beautifully, if artificially, proportioned young woman and getting shot at by same with a blank plus paint pellet in the face, I was interested in committing further murders. I told him that I was on again that very night.

Excellent, he said, wincing a little. I asked him what was wrong. He said Tulip had been "drawing" on him. That the drawings—there were more than one of them—were rather large. That I could see them when they were finished, that they didn't look like much just now.

Do you think it's going to be the knockout again? Because I'd love to take another crack at killing her.

The knockout? he said. That's actually quite funny and rather appropriate, isn't it, my boy? he said. I am told that she very much enjoys applying the odd blunt object to people's nerve endings when she invites them into unconsciousness at the end of her sessions.

That's a different kind of knockout than the one I was talking about, I said.

Of course, Henry, he said.

He then said that, even in the case of trial runs, of little tests, as mine had been, Cornelius observed a strict one-murder-per-victim rule. Cornelius was not interested in fetishists. They tended to be somewhat too public about their pastimes.

He told me he murdered you.

I suppose that in a manner of speaking that is true. One could also argue that it was a collaborative effort, a joint exertion. That we both sped me into the other world. But no matter.

How long has he been doing this?

In its current incarnation, it's a fairly recent development, at least as these things go. My murder, however, the one that planted the seed, occurred a very long time ago.

When you were still living in Cooperstown?

Yes. It must have been.

Mr. Kindt's voice drifted off a little at the end of this and we sat in a silence that lasted until Mr. Kindt let out a soft belch then said excuse me.

Certainly, I said. Then I asked if Cornelius ever got up to anything besides show murders.

Mr. Kindt laughed, then stopped laughing, then let his thin little lips resolve into the position they had held earlier.

Because Anthony said last night he was just supposed to deliver a warning, but that it turned into a murder.

Mr. Kindt's lips didn't move.

What kind of murder was it—the kind I'm getting involved with and just had done to me, or the other kind? I asked.

Ask me something else, dear boy, he said.

It didn't have anything to do with those guys we bumped into at the Indian restaurant that time, did it?

Mr. Kindt looked confused for a moment, then burst out laughing and said, *really,* Henry! What sort of a person do you take me for?

I told him, in so many words, that I took him for a friend.

That's absolutely right. I am your friend. Now enough of such silliness. We've already established that, with my help, Cornelius murdered me long ago and, as you can see, I'm still very much here.

He bent his arm, held it up, and gestured for me to feel it. I did. It was surprisingly firm and definitely there.

Wow, I said.

Mr. Kindt said that although his general state of health was catastrophic and needed constant surveillance, there had been some slight holdover from his younger days.

When you were a champion swimmer.

I used to slice the water like a serrated spoon.

Is there anything else?

I'm not following you, dear boy.

I don't know. Friends tell each other things.

Like what?

Like who they are.

But you already know.

I'd love to hear it again.

I am Aris Kindt. I am a businessman. I am Dutch though it has been many years since I have visited those flat lands. I have lived in the city almost longer than I can remember. I keep interesting company. I am old and have health issues. My passions vary. I love art. I love a good bit of fish. I am not against meat. And I am not against helping young ne'er-do-wells who have lost their way and might otherwise end up in the proverbial ditch.

He crossed his arms and leaned back in his chair.

I'm sorry for that last bit—that was unnecessary, he said.

I deserved it, I said. You've been very generous. I think it's just this headache. And all this talk about murder.

Drink some more tea. I'm sure the aspirin will begin doing its job any minute. Aspirin is a wonderful drug. We tend to forget just how effective it is.

I took another drink.

Mr. Kindt apologized again for his comment. I told him again that it was all right, that the tone of my voice had risen without my being aware of it and that I had probably sounded shrill. Mr. Kindt said that I hadn't sounded shrill, only a touch insistent, and he had always had a hard time with insistence, although he both appreciated and respected it and possessed more than a drop of it himself. It was only natural that I would have questions.

In fact, ask me another question, he said. I shouldn't have cut you off.

You're sure?

He nodded.

On the same subject?

Of course.

I thought for a minute.

O.K., why is Cornelius doing this?

Because there is a market for it, certainly, and because he is a businessman. One who knows an opportunity when he sees it and has learned through the rigors of experience to leap when he does.

Like you.

Oh, yes, in many ways. Except perhaps that I never had to learn that particular lesson—that one I knew from the start.

I poured myself some more tea and, while I asked him more questions and he gave me more answers, thought about that one for a while. I decided that, despite the fact that Cornelius wore a hunting cape and said mildly strange stuff and ran a mock and maybe also not-mock murder service, he probably wasn't really all that much like Mr. Kindt. To use the knockout's term, it was a question of degree. Mr. Kindt had his own category. I didn't quite know what that category was, but then I didn't really know much of anything.

Tulip around today? I asked.

She was earlier. I think she has gone out. I'm sure she'll be along.

He was right. About five minutes later she walked through the door, went straight across the living room without saying a word to either of us, and disappeared into Mr. Kindt's bedroom.

Nap time, I said.

Mr. Kindt smiled.

She does so love to sleep, he said.

He then leaned forward and asked me if I wouldn't mind returning to the subject of murder, that once one was on it, and had gotten over one's misplaced touchiness, it was hard to stop. Mock murder, he said, could be quite instructive, could help to prepare me, to lend an air of authenticity that would spill over into all aspects of my life, that authenticity even in mock matters was very important, etc.

What about mock authenticity in real matters? I asked him.

That is an interesting question, but perhaps one for another time, he said.

He then asked what the previous night's murder weapon had been. I told him. He asked me where I had inflicted the fatal wound. I told him that the fatal wound, a poorly executed zigzag pattern, had involved the throat.

And was there any element of torture involved?

No, I said, in theory it was a clean killing.

Ah, said Mr. Kindt, his voice suddenly dreamy, as was mine.

You mean in Cooperstown? With Cornelius?

Mr. Kindt didn't answer.

Instead he said, yes, a good clean killing involving the neck and the windpipe, hung in the morning and delivered in the afternoon, and harrowed that night.

Harrowed?

In front of an audience, a learned audience, a group of wealthy spectators, led by a most famous doctor, one who with scalpel and illustrative anatomic manual devoured me. Then it was no longer clean. Then it became, in its combination of spectacle and fervid speculation, quite blurred.

Are you talking about your namesake or the namesake of your namesake? I said.

Finish your tea, my young mock murderer, he said. I feel like talking now, not conversing, perhaps there will be some sense in what I say, please listen to me.

How do you picture death? he asked. Is it a bullet released, perhaps at random, from a mile away, or a bright missile or a balloon out of which a bomb is dropped, or a knife onto which your name has been carved, or a fuel-filled airliner, or an avalanche of lava pouring through the heart of a city, or a bear's embrace, or a great flood, or a devastating cyclone? Is it a heart that has begun, after many years, to leak, or that has never worked properly, that has been replaced, perhaps, by a simulacrum, or arteries, those dark, sweeping corridors that have begun to clog? Is it a fall from a high and perhaps burning building or from a fence onto your neck or is it a fall within a funicular and you are surrounded by screams? Is disease present, has a virus, have beautifully breeding bacteria, has cellular decay, taken hold? Are you alone? Are you in a dark room alone? Is it late at night and have you drunk bleach and is it spilling out of your mouth, eating away at the soft tissue of your throat and lips? Did it happen today or long ago? Were you, along with what you had hoped was an appropriately padded barrel, swept over the edge of Niagara Falls, or did you, one fine morning in the Middle Ages, accidentally ride your horse into a tree? The Lady of Shalott died of despair. In fact, many, very many, have died of despair, and it is important to point out that although it is poetic to think so, it is not the heart but the brain that gives out. And what of the tiny blood vessels, the small bearers of blood? You are young, you are surrounded by your fellows, you are on your way into Nazareth for the market and some great spectacle two thousand years ago, and such a vessel explodes in your brain. And there are other ways.

One can be hung, he said, beheaded, disemboweled, racked, flogged, broken on the wheel. One could fill a tome with descriptions of all the different shapes and sharpnesses of blades that have been applied in direct or indirect anger, but also accidentally, to the flesh. One can be electrocuted, injected with chemicals, hammered to death. In Japan there was the death of a thousand cuts and in China, until quite recently, one could be killed quite slowly, in a fog of opium, by dismemberment. And then, too, it is possible to kill people while they remain alive.

I asked him what he meant by this.

He spoke then of slaves, of Samos and the tunnel of Pisistratus, of Athens and the silver mines, of Egypt and the pyramids, of the Yucatecan monuments and bone-filled *cenotes,* of the American South and its plantations, of Estaban Gomez, the black Portuguese pilot, who between the brief visit of Verrazano and the arrival of the Dutch took his boat many miles up what he called the Deer and would soon be called the Noort and was now called the Hudson, who brought back fifty-seven native inhabitants for the slave markets in Lisbon. He spoke to me of the Pygmy, taken from the former Belgian colony in Africa and kept for many months, at times with an orangutan that held him tenderly in its arms, in a cage at the Bronx zoo, and of the Sioux warriors, once at home on the endless plains of Nebraska, being paid a pittance to act like "Indians" on a modified dog track in Buffalo Bill's heralded Wild West Show. I, myself, he said, have felt at times the world becoming very far away and quite reduced and very cold, and while the doctors may have a word for it, I know it is the other thing.

He went on. On and on, talking to me as I sat there watching him and as Tulip slept in the other room, about death and destruction, which words, he said, were simply abstractions of all of these things and the final quieting of the heart, and that these things, these emphatic messengers, were endless, and that our representations of them had fueled rite and ritual since before our ancestors had stopped using their teeth to hold animal hide, and that, while many had sung of the great variety of life, of its rich and fulsome plenitude, if asked to stand and take his turn at the great song of being, he would sing of death and its agents, bright and dark, alone or in company, mock or real, on the earth or in the air or below the seas.

SIXTEEN

My dentist has a very nice office near Washington Square,
and my dentist is very nice. I better say this in the past
tense—obviously, my dentist is no longer my dentist. She
did, or rather would do, my teeth. She had a lovely by-the-
reclining-chair manner and lovely calming eyes and her
hands were tiny with fingers that could fit easily into your
mouth. Her articulations were extraordinarily sensitive; even
with latex covering her fingertips she could feel slight rough-
nesses on rear molars or gauge the severity of abrasions
afflicting the gums. Also, she had a very relaxed payment
plan, so relaxed that I was actually able to have a tremendous amount of work done without ever paying much for
it. Every now and again, before I lost my apartment, I
would receive a blue envelope with a request, from her
office, for some money. Never all of the money, just some.
I would ignore these requests, though not the envelopes—
those I kept in an ever-growing pile in a little wooden box
under a pile of miscellaneous domestic accumulation by the
bedroom door. Carine did some sorting one day, found the
box, and got suspicious. And proceeded to let me know it.
With such eventual insistence that I eventually, in her presence, threw all the little blue envelopes away, then, still in
her presence, carried out the trash and threw it into the can
outside. This of course didn't stop me, a little later, from

retrieving them, from carrying them over to a bar, having a few Cape Cods, and going through them again. Or from following my dentist home once.

She walked very slowly, going in and out of small stores, acquiring an ever-increasing number of plastic bags. And there I went behind her, encountering an impressive array of stores and shops I had previously been unfamiliar with, some of which I visited the following day. They were establishments in which, I discovered, one could make quality purchases, if one was so inclined and had the wherewithal. I myself purchased, so to speak, a bottle of coriander-scented hand lotion, which, out of a general sense of guilt for indulging in pointless obsessive behavior, I took home for Carine. This offering, incidentally, did nothing to assuage my guilty feelings, not least because Carine reminded me that the hand lotion I had chosen was both the brand and scent she had wrinkled her elegant nose at when we had gone out shopping the previous week.

When we arrived at my dentist's building, I watched her disappear through handsome smoked-glass double doors as I leaned—both nervous and contented—against a lamppost. There is a curious, unquantifiable pleasure to be had in following someone home to a skyscraper, even a relatively short one. It was difficult, pleasantly so, to correlate that building, which I could only have seen all of from a considerable distance, with my dentist, whose hands and surrounding body were so small. As I leaned against my lamppost, I imagined her inhabiting whole floors of the building, palatial spaces through which she would move languorously, accomplishing tiny, mysterious tasks, looking around her as she went with wonder, satisfaction, awe.

In retrospect, as I have lain here listening to Hank Williams or to Mr. Kindt or to Dr. Tulp, i.e., while my present bleeds all over my past, this image has changed for me. Or rather another image has presented itself and vies for my attention as I think of leaning against the lamppost, looking up at the face of her building. In this competing image, my dentist, far from inhabiting whole floors, lives in an apartment the size of a closet. She has mounted hooks on the walls and on them hang all of her possessions, including the contents of the plastic bags she has most lately brought home. She cannot quite stand up in this closet-sized apartment. She has to take deep breaths to get any good out of the stale air. She sits very still on a chair in the center of all the hooks and hanging objects. Every now and again her hand goes out and brings something back to put in her mouth. Sometimes it is just the hand itself. The hand goes out then enters her mouth. Eventually, she falls asleep.

Still, what it is about the dentist I wanted to relate does not primarily concern the blue envelopes or following her home or the claustrophobic variants thereon that my memory has lately been offering up. It's this—once it wasn't she who worked on me. It was an associate, some guy. Now, unlike hers, this associate's hands were very large, and his fingers were sort of spatulate, and he wasn't too convincing with the tools. And his own teeth, on top of that, weren't, let's say, so nifty. In fact, more than a few of said teeth were dark brown. I think you'll agree that nobody wants that kind of dentist. And as a matter of fact I told him so. He asked me, as a counter, if I had read the *Odyssey,* and after looking at him with eyebrow raised for a minute I said that I had. He asked me which translation and I told him I couldn't call it to mind.

Ah, he said.

What are you talking about? I said.

Nobody. You said Nobody wants that kind of dentist. I thought you were making a literary reference.

Well, I wasn't.

We had a little more back-and-forth and then he said, suit yourself. But at this point we were still midtreatment and my tooth was killing me. So I let him pull it, which he didn't do too tenderly, and I left.

That evening I saw my friend Fish, a character, at the bar, and he said, how are you? and I said shitty, and he said why? and I pointed at my mouth and said, dentist. A drink or two later Fish told me a story.

He said, I had a creepy dentist once. Kind of like yours, only his teeth weren't brown, they were fake. Supposedly he had abused his teeth pretty badly in his youth and after he lost them he saw the light and became a dentist. Kind of an oral-fixation born-again thing. Anyway, my creepy dentist, after he had done some shit to me without any pain-suppressing substance having been applied, put a needle-tipped jackhammer in my mouth and told me this anecdote: Once he had a dream. In the dream an angel with excellent choppers informed him that if he only dug deep enough he would find the answer to all his questions inside one of his future client's teeth.

I don't like this story, Fish, I said.

Fine, said Fish.

And we talked about something else. Since this something else was pretty interesting, and because it bolsters my contention that Fish was a character, I will include it here. What we talked about was where Fish was currently living. Or squatting.

Fish was a big squatter. Until fairly recently, Fish, who had once held down a boring but remuneratively satisfactory job as a copy editor that allowed him to inhabit a dingy one-bedroom in Chinatown, had proudly lived in a squat on East Sixth. The owners of the building, unable to get the squatters to leave, had decided to tear the building down. Fish had been the last to leave. He had been, as they say, forcibly removed. But not before making a minor celebrity of himself in the squatter and friends-of-squatters communities by standing completely naked on the fire escape, sort of dancing around and singing what I heard from other sources was a pretty decent operatic tenor version first of "Imagine," then of "Rhinestone Cowboy."

He had a new squat now. A big two-bedroom on Fourth between B and C. Or actually, as he explained, it was more of a share. When he moved in, it had been a squat, because the owner, according to the tip he had received, was supposedly dead and there was no next of kin and the city had no immediate plans. A key had been under the mat and there was some furniture (including a sinkful of unwashed but perfectly usable dishes) and the electricity hadn't been cut off: paradise. He thought about letting a couple of his colleagues from the demolished squat in on his find but decided to keep a low profile for a while. Which was a good thing. Because the owner wasn't dead. He came in the second evening as Fish was flossing his teeth on the couch: an old guy in a beat-up porkpie. Fish stopped stock-still with the piece of floss between a pair of molars. The old guy, however, did not appear to see Fish, who was sitting very much in plain sight. This was because, as Fish quickly gathered, the old guy was blind. He was also, apparently, extremely hard of hearing. Fish had spotted a monstrous pair of hearing aids by the bed in the room he had not chosen to sleep in and the old guy's ears were currently unencumbered. Fish stood up, very slowly, and went and leaned against the wall farthest away from the door. The old guy, who had not removed his beat-up porkpie, immediately started puttering around in the kitchen and singing to himself. He did the dishes, which Fish had added to, and he put away everything that was on the counter. Fish thought about getting his stuff and making his getaway while the old guy did his thing around the kitchen, but instead he kept leaning against the wall, and when he finally moved after the old man had gone into the bathroom and started a shower, it was just to go into the little room he had chosen and to go to sleep.

He still doesn't know I'm there, said Fish.

I don't believe you, I said. I don't believe a word.

I'm pretty discreet and if I see he's got his hearing aids in I don't move.

What, he can't smell either?

The guy's ancient. Plus he's always cooking. He likes spicy food.

You're full of shit.

I keep my stuff under the bed.

You're squatting in a guy's place and the guy still lives there.

Like I said, it's more of a share. Anyway, there's weirder shit going on.

Which of course is true, and you don't have to look very far to come up with examples. As a matter of fact I immediately thought, as Fish said this, of the story I had read that week about a woman who had kept the remains of her dead child in a box in a closet for twenty years. The extra-creepy part was that she had two other kids and they had grown up in the apartment with the remains of their sibling in a box in their mother's room. Then there was the guy in the Bronx who kept a tiger as a pet. When the tiger started to get surly the owner moved out, returning daily to toss meat in to it. The neighbors heard roaring along with "odd thumping noises" but didn't, they said, give it too much thought.

Anyway, not long after my experience with the unpleasant substitute dentist and subsequent conversation with Fish, my regular dentist informed me in a rather lengthy and unfortunately detailed phone message, which Carine listened to before I returned home, that I could no longer come to her office, that I could no longer set foot on her premises, that if I came back or followed her again she would call the police.

The blue envelopes became white envelopes from a collection agency. Then they became collection agents, joining the other collection agents, not to mention some of my former friends, including Fish, in pounding on my door.

One afternoon shortly after Aunt Lulu's visit, I told Mr. Kindt some of what I have just related, including the anecdote regarding teeth, and he said, what did the dentist do? I said I didn't know, because I hadn't let Fish finish his story.

What kind of name is Fish? asked Mr. Kindt. Is it short for something? Fischbach or Fischstein or Fischman, perhaps?

I don't know, I said.

It's a very nice name, he said.

I thought you would like it.

I would like to be called Fish, said Mr. Kindt. Perhaps under other circumstances I would ask you to call me that.

He smiled. I thought about Fish and about calling Mr. Kindt, who cried when he thought of fish but not when he ate them, Fish, and smiled too.

But it is a shame that you didn't permit him to finish his story, it is a promising beginning.

Is it?

It is. In the Leiden of my earlier days there was just such a dentist who had just such a dream.

There were dentists in those days?

After a fashion.

And how did his story end?

I don't know, when I was told it the teller was called away before he could continue past the point where the soon crazed dentist takes a mallet to a young woman's tooth.

Maybe it's the same story, I said.

Likely, said Mr. Kindt. Many stories without clear endings are the same.

This remark made me think of Aunt Lulu and of a series of unpleasant afternoons many years before. It also made me think of Dr. Tulp, who that morning had told me I might soon be moving on and that the nature of our relationship would consequently change.

Change how? I had said.

Dr. Tulp hadn't answered.

Do you mean that things between us might become more amicable?

Don't you think they are quite amicable now?

I mean *more* amicable.

Dr. Tulp had smirked and shaken her head.

So am I better?

I'm not sure it's useful at this juncture to think in terms of better or not better.

This is because of my aunt, right?

Do you feel like discussing your aunt now?

No, thanks.

Then we won't.

So what will we discuss?

Dr. Tulp had looked at me, long and hard. She had crossed her legs and uncrossed them. She had lifted her clipboard and written something on it. She had stopped looking at me and looked at the clock over the whiteboard she sometimes used for drawing diagrams. She liked to use different colored markers for her diagrams. There were bits of violet, red, green, and blue ghosting the white surface. In one corner it was still possible to make out the remains of the adapted Greimas square she had used at a previous session to discuss opposites (life/death) and negatives (not-life/not-death) and the way these binaries interacted every time we said something. A reference to Gondola Bus Lines appeared to have figured into the discussion. I said "Gondola Bus Lines" aloud. For the second time. The first time having prompted her explanation of the diagram. This time she just nodded and tapped two long white fingers on the armrest of her chair.

I think we're done for the day, Henry, she said.

I'm not sure I like this stories-without-endings thing, I told Mr. Kindt.

No, said Mr. Kindt, neither am I. Fortunately, many stories do have endings, even if they aren't nice ones.

The last thing I have to say, in this connection, is that once as I was walking near the smoking rubble downtown I heard a guy say, with great depth and seriousness, my friends, it is my great delight to reveal to you that it is either a Ritz or it is a Saltine, and because I wasn't in any big hurry, I stopped and asked him what "it" was.

The answer, he said.

That is the story of my teeth. The story of my life is different, though, and even if it is not entirely coherent, even if some parts have been elided into others, it does have a beginning, a middle, and an end.

The End.

I hope that is how simple it will be.

SEVENTEEN

At 3 a.m. I went to the address on St. Mark's Place and, after climbing six flights of stairs this time, was greeted by Cornelius when I walked through the unlocked door. He was wearing his hat and hunting cape, but was otherwise not particularly elegant in speech or action that night.

Am I supposed to murder *you*? I asked, huffing a little.

No, Henry, he said, lifting a gloved hand and pointing over his shoulder with it, the victim is in the next room.

Are the contortionists here?

We're all here, he said.

What does that mean?

Ça veut dire qu'on est tous ensemble.

You speak French?

He shrugged.

I used to date someone who spoke French. I mean, she was practically French. Have you been over there? She liked this place called Chartres. For the light pouring through its rose windows and the maze painted on its floor. She had a long story about how she liked to sit outside in the evening light and watch the swallows swoop around its flying buttresses, hunting insects. We were supposed to go over there together. Paris. Marseilles. Chartres. All that.

Cornelius didn't respond. I looked around. I didn't see anyone else. It was a tiny front room, barely big enough for a coffee table and the little yellow couch Cornelius was now sitting on. Behind him on the wall was an interesting picture in a brushed-silver frame. Concentric rings drew the eye into a cloud of intersecting lines in the center. To get there you had to go through a number of color combinations: yellow gave way to green-yellow gave way to salmon then to salmon-gray then gray-silver then gray-yellow, etc., to dizzying effect. The smooth-edged somewhat irregular outer rings looked to have been laid down by hand with colored pencil, while the mesh-textured inner rings looked a little like they had been created with Spirographs, those grooved plastic drawing rings that were in vogue in my childhood, and that I used a few times at a friend's house, though it goes without saying that the results were nothing like this.

Do you know who that's by? I said.

Cornelius clicked his tongue, looked over his shoulder, then back at me.

I don't live here, Henry, he said.

That's a shame, because it's pretty great.

Cornelius turned and looked at it again, this time a little more closely.

I would say it's by Emma Kunz. It's a reproduction.

Who lives here?

Some people, they cleared out for a couple of hours.

Do they have any more of these?

They have some stuff.

Cornelius said this with just enough edge to indicate that he wasn't interested in discussing art with me any further. I couldn't quite tell though if the implied request for me to stop speaking was a general one, and because I hadn't yet been told what I was supposed to do, I tried changing the subject.

So you've known Mr. Kindt for a long time? I said.

Yes, Henry. Like I said, we go way back.

All the way back to Cooperstown.

Cornelius had been examining his fingernails. He looked up at me.

It must have been something, that swim he took.

Cornelius nodded. It was quite a swim. You could say that swim took him all the way to New York. All the way to where he is now.

He told me this afternoon that he'd done it with his arms tied behind his back.

Did he now?

He was kidding.

Cornelius shrugged, then said, Aris Kindt. Nice name, isn't it? Not the average. Has some splash to it. Kind of name you'd like to try on and take for a spin around the block. Fits him doesn't it? To a т. You'd look at him and say, now that is a guy who has got the right fucking name. Has a ring.

I said I agreed but that I liked the name Cornelius too, and Cornelius said, I'm happy for you, now, please, Henry, there is work to do, shut the fuck up.

I started to speak, but Cornelius shook his head, put his finger to his lips, pointed to a slip of paper on the coffee table, then pointed to the door leading into the next room.

Can we talk afterward? I said.

Shhh, Cornelius said. I'm not kidding.

I picked up the piece of paper, opened the door, and went into a surprisingly long hallway lit by a series of night-lights plugged into sockets placed at regular intervals near the floor along each wall. When I was about halfway down the hall-way, the door I had just come through opened again.

Expecting Cornelius, I turned and found myself looking at the contortionists. I began to greet them, but they came up quickly and, smiling, began poking and tickling and prodding me forward. When we got to the end of the hallway one of them slipped past me, pushed open the other door, and swept her hand out as if to say, here it is. The other gave my shoulders a few rubs, shoved me forward through the doorway, then jumped past me and stood next to her colleague. They both put mock serious looks on their faces, did a little shadowboxing, gave me the thumbs-up, then flipped themselves over and scuttled back down the hallway and out the door.

The room I entered was larger and more elaborately furnished than I had expected given the street, the general condition of the building, and the Spartan aesthetic that presided in the front room and hallway. There was plush wall-to-wall, deep-shag burgundy carpeting, a long black couch, a good-looking leather cigar chair, a zinc bar with a couple of mahogany stools, a large retro refrigerator and a backlit row of top-shelf bottles, floor lamps that gave off red and gold highlights, and, though there weren't any more Emma Kunz—or whoever it was—reproductions, at least not in this room, there were two or three expensively framed posters. One of these was a blown-up extra-handsome comic strip featuring a mustachioed heavyset older man with a camera around his neck. Another was a famous black-and-white aerial shot of the Flatiron building taken in the thirties or forties. It wasn't difficult, looking at the scene from beyond even the photographer's elevated vantage point, which had reduced all the human beings present to the size and relative significance of dust motes, to feel myself shrinking too. I liked this feeling. New York is interesting in that even at the bottom of the skyscrapers' deepest trenches a good portion of its inhabitants tend to feel a little bigger, a little more consequential, than they are. In fact, there are days and nights when it feels like everyone (and maybe this is what I meant before about East Villagers looking fat) is holding out oversize thumbs in hopes that history, like some gargantuan stretch limo, will slam on its brakes for them. Not (my comments about being overweight myself to the contrary) me. I've always been plenty happy to believe that history would just blow on past if it saw me standing there with my suitcase. On one of our first outings, Mr. Kindt referred to history as "that vast dark entity ravaged by loss and erasure." Exactly. Not the kind of thing you want stopping for you. It was while I was standing in front of this poster, thinking it was just fine that buildings and trees and cars are the only things that can be seen with any clarity from a distance, that Tulip walked into the room.

She was wearing a long dark-blue silk robe and sequined house slippers and more makeup than I'd ever seen on her, dark around the mouth and eyes. The script Cornelius had handed me read "Keep your mouth shut, watch and improvise," so I didn't say anything, just kind of took her in as she sauntered toward me holding what looked a lot like a hatchet.

Later, she told me it was an eighteenth-century embalming tool she had borrowed from Mr. Kindt. This was after Tulip had woken up and we had all walked out together— Cornelius, the contortionists, the knockout, me, and Tulip; after Cornelius had said, good, but I have nothing to say to you about speaking French or art or our mutual friend, and the knockout had said, who would've thought? and the contortionists had said nothing, though they had both given me another thumbs-up and one had kissed and kind of nibbled at the other's arm. The two of us had repaired to a nearby after-hours establishment at Tulip's suggestion, an invitation that prompted me to register, with more than moderate trepidation, that I had begun my very long day by being summoned to the Odessa by the knockout, my first victim, and that I was ending it with my second.

You're not going to give me some advice then ruin my shirt and hurt my eardrums are you? I said after we'd left the others.

No more advice necessary, she said. You heard Cornelius.

Not only had I heard Cornelius, Cornelius had given me two hundred more smackeroos.

I'll buy, I said.

I was expecting you to.

We took a seat in the back of the comfortably shabby place, with its wooden floors, hammered metal ceiling, and soft Nordic jazz, and Tulip said, that was impressive, very direct, very to the point, how did you come up with it?

I don't know, I said. I improvised.

Which was true.

I also said, after a minute, and there was this drawing in the lobby. Cornelius and I were checking it out before things got started. All these rings and lines leading into the middle. I guess that made me think I should try something interesting but, as you put it, direct. Plus there were the two, you know, contortionist friends, pushing me forward and rubbing my shoulders and knocking a few shadow punches around, like I was heading into the ring. There was also a poster of the Flatiron building that got me going a little on how history doesn't so much hate us as blindly devour us, like a growing whale eating plankton, so I must have thought a little, maybe just in the back of my mind, of devouring you.

Which was all also true and, I thought, interesting. But Tulip just said, yeah? The "yeah?" she used when she hadn't listened to what you had just said.

We drank in silence for a little while, then I tried some flattery.

You looked good in that robe, I said.

She smiled or smirked—it was too dark to tell which—but didn't say anything.

I thought I'd better try something else.

So you're involved too, I said.

She shook her head. Not really. Cornelius just asked me to help out tonight.

Did he ask you in French?

No. I don't *parlez français*. Do you?

No. I know a few words. I used to date someone who was fluent. Did he pay you?

She shook her head—it was a favor. That's why you're buying. Go buy more.

I went over to the bar and bought us another round.

It seems like a pretty questionable gimmick, I said when I got back to the table. I mean, do they have people who actually want to pay to have that done to them?

Tulip shrugged. It's the times, she said. It's in the air. Gloom and doom. New York–style. Aris says it falls under the rubric of the *danse macabre*.

That's French.

So is the Statue of Liberty, honey. Not to mention Dior and cognac. Would you like to hear some Latin?

Are you serious?

Spiritus meus attenuabitur, dies mei breviabuntur.

What the fuck does that mean?

"My spirit is corrupt, my breath grows extinct." It's from the Bible. I saw it in one of Aris's books. Ask him to show it to you. It's mostly a picture book. Full of skeletons and people doing the danse macabre. Mostly the skeletons are doing the dancing. "Ring around the Rosie" is more or less what we're talking about.

I raised an eyebrow.

"Ashes, ashes, we all fall down!" A danse macabre for kids growing up in plague times.

I heard that wasn't true. That it didn't have anything to do with the plague.

Whatever. It's true enough. Can you think of anything?

Dead man's float, I said, remembering once bobbing face-down in the water at the Hamilton Fish Park pool long enough for the lifeguard to jump in.

Or just playing dead. It's all the same thing. The closer you think you are to death, even if you haven't thought about it, the more you . . .

Danse? I said.

Yeah. And anyway, people pay to have all kinds of bizarre and/or anodyne shit done to them.

Like what?

Like hair implants, collagen injections, liposuction, skin lightening, complexion alteration, extreme makeovers, safaris, Rolfing.

Do you think the knockout . . . ?

The what?

Never mind. It's stupid. Any idea why Mr. Kindt wants me involved?

Who knows, you never know with Aris. Maybe Cornelius

told him he needed a new guy. I understand that pretty boy from last night isn't going to work out.

You mean Anthony?

Is that what you call him?

Pretty boy? I said.

The knockout? she said.

Tulip did the smile/smirk thing again. I sagged a little into my chair.

Don't worry, Henry, you're pretty too, she said.

Yeah? I said, the way I quietly say it when someone has just told me something I'd like to hear again. I leaned back, then forward, then cleared my throat.

But she just shook her head and told me about the blade, that it was a kind of scalpel, once owned by a famous Dutch embalmer, that Mr. Kindt owned the embalmer's entire set of tools.

It's an impressive little collection, she said. You should ask Aris to show it to you when you look at the danse macabre book.

Do you think he brought it down with him from Cooperstown?

Maybe, she said. But I was under the impression that he was pretty broke when he hit town. I'm guessing he got it, like most of his stuff, when things started picking up.

Do you really think I'm pretty? I said.

I do, she said.

With that she got up and walked out the door.

I stayed another hour, playing the murder scene over, again and again, comparing it with the mess from the night before. I thought about how I had taken Tulip down not so much *onto* as *into* the plush carpet—hard but not too hard—how I had put my forearm against her throat and pulled her forehead back, how she had gasped and grinned madly and looked into my eyes, then passed out. How the knockout and contortionists had emerged for a moment, taken in the scene, then withdrawn.

I'm pretty, I thought. I ended this little colloquy with myself by letting my head fall to my chest, my shoulders droop, and my mouth sag open.

Danse macabre, New York–style, I said.

I repeated this the next day when I went over to Mr. Kindt's. He did his own version, one that involved shutting his eyes, sucking in his cheeks, and leaning back into his chair. Then he told me that he too liked to play dead, and that once he had had to play dead to stay alive when a business affair he had been involved with had gone "terribly wrong."

It was so strange, he said, to have a pulse when those around me did not, to have hands and feet and toes I could still wiggle when those around me did not, to be able, after those long minutes, to rise and leave when those around me could not.

I had more or less not stopped playing dead while he spoke. When he had finished, I opened my eyes and looked at him. He was sitting up straight with his arms folded over his chest, looking at me.

The episode I just described did not happen, he said. But I have often imagined such a scenario and it is true that I like to play dead.

And you've been murdered before.

He smiled. He suggested we play dead a little longer. While I was still lying there with my eyes shut he put a cracker in my hand and asked if I would like a cup of hot tea.

EIGHTEEN

One gray morning, Job walked into my room and said, get rid of it.

I nodded, and Job walked out.

An hour or so later, after I had taken the little case of vials and the white robe with its ID badge to the incinerator chute—burning my hand on the chute's handle in the process—he came back.

He said, we've got difficulties—they called the cops after that last one.

Yeah? I said.

So we stop. Call a temporary halt until things quiet down. It should be O.K., all good, you know, but keep cool. They talk to you, you don't know anything, right?

I remember, I said.

Job went away. I never saw him again. The next day I heard from a new nurse that he had gotten himself picked up walking out of his apartment door with a suitcase and a fat wallet, had made some commentary, and had gotten smacked a couple of times, before being encouraged to kiss the pavement while he was cuffed.

I was sure I was next. In fact, I could practically hear them coming down the hall, a whole lot of them, probably more than was necessary. Since they were about to arrive at any second, I tried to get myself in the right frame of mind to be hauled off, imagining how I would act (tough, impervious) and what I would say (nothing) and what kind of look (devil-may-care, baby) I would give Dr. Tulp, standing in the door of the hospital as they shoved me into the car, and to Mr. Kindt, standing beside her (noble, resigned), and what I would do to Job (unmentionable) when I saw him, if I saw him.

For a couple of days (they didn't come), I ran through a lot of permutations of this basic scenario, permutations that got pretty strange when I'd get my meds. I won't get into all of them, because that would just be too boring, but, as an example, in one I hugged Mr. Kindt, who had very awful, very fishy breath, then kicked Dr. Tulp's shin as the police were dragging me away.

Mr. Kindt, you're my friend, Dr. Tulp, I hate you, I called as they stuffed me into the waiting patrol car.

It would probably be only fair to note, as a kind of corrective to the above-expressed sentiment, that most of the permutations in fact only involved Dr. Tulp. I mean there were no police and there was no Mr. Kindt and no hospital in them, and believe me, I wasn't kicking shins. I was both elegant and gallant as I escorted Dr. Tulp to various local purveyors of handsome vintage apparel so that she could appropriately outfit herself for her upcoming green card proceedings and subsequent celebratory gatherings with her colleagues in the medical profession. At said gatherings, I would stand beside her in appropriate apparel of my own, holding a handsomely housed Cape Cod or Campari and soda, whose rich colors would add that subtle touch of depth to the convivial atmosphere. Occasionally, Dr. Tulp would flick her hand out and stab me with her pen, or lean close and sink her teeth into the soft flesh of my neck, but no one would take any notice and the smiles and soft chatter would go on and on. It is true that both Job and Mr. Kindt occasionally trespassed into these scenarios, but they invariably appeared in a service capacity, moving in and out of the crowd with trays of drinks and small, mysterious edibles encased in puffed pastry.

A few days went by like this, or maybe it was more than a few. In addition to the mental space taken up by my dismal flights of fancy, the subject of lost cats came into my mind and lodged there, unpleasantly, as did that of lost love. Thinking of this latter, I took to positioning myself on a bench by the ward's main entrance in the hope that some remnant thereof would find its way through those tall metal doors. If Aunt Lulu—whom I had lost or let go or let sink forward toward her bowl of macaroni and cheese—had found me, I reasoned, why couldn't Carine, whom I had lost in a different way but just as definitively? Dr. Tulp got concerned after I began to talk a lot about saliva in one of our sessions and upped my meds. I smacked the new nurse, an outrageously comely individual wearing a silver charm necklace with little devils on it, because the way she lifted her arm reminded me of Aunt Lulu, and passed a night in restraining straps with a slab of cold lead on my chest. Then I heard they weren't going after anyone except Job, who was wanted for a couple of other, more complicated things.

This news calmed me down to some extent, but I did spend time obsessing over what Job's other operations might have been. He'd talked one night about what had sounded at the time like a condominium deal in Florida, so I imagined him taking big, illicit bites of mob-related bogus property deals and eventually bilking the wrong guy. Because another time he had mentioned a predilection for indulging in a certain variety of late-night extracurricular activity and had remarked on its probable profitability, I pictured him running a ring of prostitutes, one catering exclusively to lower-middle-class East Village shop owners, maybe hiring someone to slip flyers under security grates at night. Job, as I imagined it, would sit at the center of this handsomely functioning mechanism with a green visor and violet glasses placing phone calls, delivering comportment lectures, and tallying receipts. When this line of thought began to lose its freshness, I decided that I needed to start getting some exercise and began jumping up and down and pumping my fists and doing other calisthenics in front of my mesh-covered window.

The new nurse came in then went out.

That is not acceptable behavior in a public facility, Henry, Dr. Tulp said.

But is it productive? I said.

It is neither productive nor acceptable, Henry. That bed you were jumping up and down on like it was your own personal property is the property of this facility and is not to be damaged. And jumping up and down without any clothes on anywhere in this facility besides your bathroom is out-of-bounds, period.

Well, fuck you.

That's not very productive either, Henry.

No, I don't suppose it fucking is, I said.

Dr. Tulp put one of her long, thin fingers on the intercom button and asked an attendant to come in. Two of them answered her call. They were small but persuasive.

That's when I started talking about Aunt Lulu.

I talked and related and described, and after a while Dr. Tulp told the attendants it was all right for them to step back.

Ah, Aunt Lulu, I said. Aunt Lulu in her dirty house-dress. Aunt Lulu with the protruding veins in her calves. Aunt Lulu and her cats before school. Big fat fucking huge and mean-as-hell Aunt Lulu.

Tell me about this meanness.

She used to kill her cats. After she had had them for a while, she would coax them into a double-ply plastic bag and seal it.

That is mean. But do you think it was inappropriate?

I thought so. I found some of them one day when I was building a fort at the back of the yard. My friend and I actually played with them for a while. The bags. We used them to build a dike.

And your father?

Long gone.

You used to own cats, didn't you?

I shook my head.

Good, Henry, she said. That's some progress, we've made some progress now.

I'm lying, I said.

What are you lying about, Henry?

About the fort. About Aunt Lulu. About everything.

Dr. Tulp's long, thin finger flicked out, and the attendants came back in when I got out of my seat and started to shout.

Mr. Kindt helped me get out of this sorry rut. One day he came into my room, tapped me on the shoulder, and took me for a little walk around the ward. When I got back I felt different, better. Actually, *better* is overstating it. Especially given the way things evolved. Maybe what I should give Mr. Kindt credit for is helping me get out of one rut and into another, and everyone knows that change, in the grand scheme of things, is rarely good.

Anyway, it was quiet time, when the doctors are off in their offices and the nurses and attendants sit quietly behind counters and the patients are in their beds, maybe thumbing through magazines or books or watching television or staring out the window, maybe mired in nightmares, awake or asleep.

We walked for a time in a silence broken only by Mr. Kindt's breathing and the soft thud of our feet. When we did fall into conversation, it was only so he could tell me about a book he had once owned and read obsessively. This fascinating work contained a list of books, artworks, and objects that in a better world would have been written, painted, crafted, or found but in this poor world of ours probably hadn't been. He had loved this list so much that he had memorized many of the descriptions, which included *A Sub Marine Herbal,* describing the several vegetables found on the rocks, hills, valleys, and meadows at the bottom of the sea; *A Tragedy of Thyestes,* and another of *Medea,* writ by Diogenes the Cy-nick; *The Prophecy of the Cathay Quail,* being the veritable and exquisite chronic of that epic questor whose exemplary fate it was never to be less than twain, by Anonymous, with engravings by Winfried Georg; *A Snow Piece,* of Land and Trees covered with snow and ice, and mountains of ice floating in the sea, with bears, seals, foxes, and variety of rare fowls upon them; and *An Etiudros Alberti* or Stone that is apt to be always moist: useful unto drie tempers, and to be held in the hand in Fevers instead of Crystal, Eggs, Limmons, Cucumbers. He gave the titles and descriptions in a kind of dreamy half-whispered cadence, which helped them to lodge more firmly in my own head, and I suspect that if he hadn't eventually pressed my arm, raised his voice, and switched the subject, being with him *would have* done me some good beyond getting me out of my rut.

As it was though, he said, well, Henry, you are quite low, quite low indeed it seems.

I looked at him and nodded.

It is the blue devil of melancholy, he said.

Must be, I said.

It is a vanquisher of kings, a destroyer of great minds, a ruiner of artists, so what can such as we hope for?

Very little, I said.

That's right. He squeezed my arm and laughed.

I asked him what he thought was funny.

We are, he said. Walking round and round a hospital ward in these awful robes.

I looked at his robe. It was covered in strange splotches and was wet in places. I tried to look at mine.

There's a documentary on tonight, he said.

On what?

North American fur traders. On the system's ever-shifting economic model, the breakthrough that was made possible when the mechanism of wampum was understood, on the types of traps they used, on the extraordinary amount of pain experienced by the beavers, gnawing away at their bloodied feet and hands.

Hands? I said.

I speak figuratively.

Have you already seen it?

Twice before.

Sounds depressing.

One blue devil for another.

I suppose.

We had entered a long, cold stretch of empty hallway, the locked doors giving onto storerooms, spare showers with handicap bars, and visitor toilets. There was a distant rattling sound somewhere in the walls and, occasionally, what sounded like a distant scream. Otherwise it was silent. Mr. Kindt paused here.

We continue, he said.

What? I said.

Just like before, except that now you get your tips directly from me.

I looked at him.

He smiled.

What do you mean now I get my tips *directly* from you? Where did they come from before?

Certainly not from Job.

Mr. Kindt smiled. It was a hard smile, hard and cold like a thin piece of frozen fruit pie. Looking at it I shivered involuntarily and thought of its owner crying about herring and standing in the shower talking about screaming. I thought about his obsession with seventeenth-century Dutch exploits, including his own, which were the product, he said, of that "vortex of Dutch-made misery whose razor edges extended to the far corners of the world," and I thought of his giggle and how he would go outside in freezing weather in his robe. I looked at his hard, cold smile and thought of these things and of other things and I shook my head and started to walk away.

Where are you going, Henry?

I'm sorry but you're—I mean this literally but in the best possible sense—crazy, Mr. Kindt. Which is fine in general, especially here, but not for business.

We're both literally crazy, Henry.

I'm not, I said over my shoulder. I got hit by a truck— I'm just traumatized. I have some dreams. Some communication issues. Pretty soon I'm getting out of here.

Hit by a truck, Henry?

Yes. A flower truck. It was my fault.

It *was* your fault, he said. It certainly was. But that was quite some time ago. It's true that you went to the hospital, a hospital for the injuries you describe, but that's not why you're here now. Oh, my, heavens no—that's most certainly not why.

I didn't answer. I started walking faster.

Come back here, Henry, Mr. Kindt shouted.

But I didn't. I went back to my room and looked out the window through the black netting or whatever it was and wondered if I would see—I did not, I did not see anything—a balloon heliuming its way up into the ether. I wondered, also, if I would ever tell Dr. Tulp the truth about Aunt Lulu, that I had stood by, without lifting a finger, when I could have helped her. But it was all too long ago to matter anyway. Wasn't it? So much else had happened. Was happening. I wondered about what I had said about being traumatized, about the possibly erroneous nature of the causal relationship of my trauma with the truck, which had been full, I suddenly remembered, though I wasn't sure why, of the pinkest lilies. I wondered also about Mr. Kindt's smile and the strange look, not entirely pleasant, that had taken over his eyes. When I thought about it, it was a little like the one that had come into them just before he had bitten my ankle so hard that, later, when he had left, I had had to ask Job for some antiseptic cream.

After a few minutes he came in. He was holding a package under his arm and a piece of paper in his hand.

Look, come on, I've had enough, stop already, I said.

Here is a hospital robe, plus fake ID, and a time frame plus parameters for the next score.

The next score? Listen to how you're talking. Who are you? I can't believe this. What next score?

The authorities needed someone, as they always do— they came and got someone. They've taken him away. He won't return. That is the way of things. This does not stop us, in any way, from continuing. Do you want a cigar? I'm dying for one.

We can't smoke in here.

We can do anything we want in here, Henry, that's the way it works, said Mr. Kindt, unwrapping one of his Dutch Masters, rolling it between his fingers, sniffing it, then lighting a match.

The way what works?

He winked. I looked at his eyes. Whatever had been in them had gone.

All right, my boy?

I looked out the window. No balloon came. No bird flew by. The sounds of the street seemed very distant. I seemed very distant. Empty circles within circles. Inertia clearly had the upper hand. I shrugged then nodded. Then looked at him. Then at the floor. It needed cleaning.

One blue devil for another, Henry, Mr. Kindt said.

NINETEEN

It was a good job, great even. Despite my skepticism, there were customers aplenty—so many that once or twice I had to turn requests down. The pay, as I've noted, was more than fair, and it quickly became clear that I could supplement it by lifting the odd item or two after I had, so to speak, put the subject away. This didn't always work out, of course. Sometimes they didn't want to stay dead. One guy, who I'd done in good with an aluminum-handled garrote, woke right up and wanted me to have a beer and maybe watch the game. In spite of myself, I found this a little strange, a touch supernatural, as if, while we were sitting there watching his plasma screen, I could see through him a little, and I didn't stay long. Another, a chipper woman who told me her friends had gotten her a murder for her thirtieth birthday, started plugging me with questions before I'd even gotten started, like about what I did in real life, what kind of music I listened to, whether I thought the murder thing was stupid, distasteful, "and/or kind of cool" (and/or kind of cool, I said), if, maybe, when we were done I'd like to take some x and "see what happens." Fortunately, the scenario I'd been given, imparted to Cornelius by her friends, had called for me to drop a good dose of her own Halcion in her drink and, in the meantime, "humor her." Which I did, and eventually her head started lolling and she shut up just before her friends were due to get there and paint her living room. Not that I minded, incidentally, at least as a concept, the x-and-possibly-getting-friendly part—it's just that, as with one or two other jobs, I had started to get the feeling I was dressed up in a Santa Claus suit and some wiseass kid was tugging on my beard.

Most of them didn't get weird or friendly though, and didn't seem to mind if I prowled around a little. A couple of times I was even *supposed* to prowl around and steal things. One woman, who told me she worked as a stock-broker in a medium-sized firm downtown as I taped her up, said I should smash what I didn't want and take the rest: it was all insured. Unfortunately there was nothing there—the requisite knickknacks, etc.—excepted, so I knocked over a lacquer vase and a row of blue coffee mugs and took a pair of toy binoculars that, when I tried them the next day, proved not to be functional, and a book I subsequently read and liked a great deal by an Italian writer, which was about black holes and supernovas and the prospect of getting stuck forever on the moon. The other time I was supposed to steal something the verbal brief was explicit. I was to murder the subject (first by knocking him out with a strong dose of chloroform, then by taking a knife from the chest of drawers in his bedroom and "being especially brutal with it") the moment he (a practicing accountant by the name of Leonard James Seligman, who worked out of his apartment by the looks of the beat-up diplomas on his wall, the big adding machine on his desk, the half-eaten sandwich, full ashtray, etc.) came home, steal his money, then bag up the entire contents of his desk's file

143 :: THE EXQUISITE

drawer (the key to which would be on his person) and ("in disgust because there is nothing there worth keeping") toss the lot into the trash outside the building. I did this, not neglecting to "act disgusted" as I feigned going through the bag before I dropped it into the garbage. It occurred to me to wonder, as I did this, if he himself had requested the murder, or if someone else, perhaps a disgruntled client, had requested it, maybe without his knowledge, for him.

I had been under the impression that the jobs would be collaborative, that the contortionists would be involved, that the knockout would stop by once in a while to add a little spice to the business, that Cornelius would occasionally climb in through a window wearing his hunting cape, but after the test runs I was left to work alone.

We're stretched too thin, Cornelius explained to me one night after I had asked him about it. Business is booming and everyone has to work.

Do you work?

I'm old, Henry. I organize—I oversee. I do other things.

Like speak French?

Cornelius raised an eyebrow.

Real murders?

No comment.

Tell me more about Mr. Kindt swimming the length of Lake Otsego on a bet.

Shut up, please.

Usually, I would get a scenario, delivered verbally—by Cornelius—a night or so before the murder, which gave me time to pick up props if they were called for and think things through a little. Sometimes, though, all I got before-hand was the time and address, with no on-site instructions waiting for me—those jobs, after I had gotten over my pre-work jitters, were probably my favorites, although the results could get a little messy, even painful.

Once, for example, the job involved a couple in a building over on Second Street, across from the old Marble Cemetery—a nice little lower-rung tenement with mosaic floors and freshly painted green stairs. I'd been buzzed in, so I figured they would open up when I knocked, but they didn't, even when I leaned close to the door and said I could hear them in there and that the meter was running and they should let me in. After a few more minutes, I knocked again, louder this time. The door next to theirs opened and a heavy old lady with greasy hair in a dirty housedress looked out. From somewhere in the apartment behind her a man's voice said, who is it, Lupe? But the old lady said nothing, just kept staring at me, with a premises-vacated-but-haunted look in her eyes. I had seen a lot of that look out in the streets and down in the subway in the eighties. Once I had woken up on one of the old plastic bucket seats in Penn Station and found someone with the look about six inches away, peering into my face.

I knocked on the couple's door.

I asked the old woman, who was still standing in her doorway, if she had the time.

She blinked, her nostrils flared slightly, she scratched her right side.

I was getting ready to leave when the husband opened the door and invited me in.

Sorry, he said. We were just getting things together. Finishing up. Come on in.

Who's the neighbor? I said.

Go back inside, Lupe, it's all right, he said.

Get back in here now, Lupe, came the man's voice from behind her.

Lupe didn't move.

Don't worry about it, she's just got a short circuit somewhere, he said.

I'm not worried, I said.

He vanished back into his apartment and, after I had said good-bye to Lupe, who did not answer, I followed him in. He introduced me to his wife. We all shook hands. They had some dinner—chicken with wild rice, salad, and sweet potatoes—going and suggested I join them. I sat down. Not too long into dinner—which wasn't bad, although the chicken was a little tough—we got to it. It was when the wife, who had just finished her glass of 2000 Long Island Blanc Fumé, said, so this is the guy that's been writing me those letters, Billy. Here he is. I wanted you to see him face-to-face. See who your competition is.

What? the husband said.

Yeah, what? I said. I wondered what I was supposed to have written. Maybe the imagined letters had been vulgar, full of details about what I'd do to her if I got her alone, etc. Or maybe they had just been enthusiastic, full of exclamation points, exciting interrogations, curlicues of banal but nicely turned supposition. Who knows what the mind wants, what it needs to talk itself into waking up. She looked nice. Pretty in a quiet, self-contained way. Like a lamp turned on in the early evening, or a modest triangle of green space on a crowded street.

The husband, for his part, did not look all that nice, though he had been pleasant enough through dinner. A tattoo of a wildly burning pinecone on his forearm had figured in the conversation. He told me he had gotten it during a stint as a construction worker in Jersey City. While sometimes, now that he wasn't working a jackhammer, he regretted having had it done, other times it filled him with a kind of pride. More than once, "on that day they got us," when he was helping with the stretchers, he had looked at it through the smoke, gritted his teeth, and soldiered on. Also, his wife found it cute.

A pinecone, she had said, as if by way of confirmation.

Listen, asshole, he said, standing up.

It didn't take a genius to figure out that now a struggle would ensue, things would get out of hand. I would kill the husband, and maybe even the wife.

All right, I said. We got to it. The trouble was the husband was more into grappling than I was, and before I knew it I was getting slapped around pretty handsomely. After a while, in fact, it was either do something drastic or give them a refund. Fortunately, the guy stopped and pointed at the big wooden salad bowl on the table. I picked it up and broke it over his head.

Sweet Jesus, God in heaven, said the wife.

Yeah, I said, starting to move toward her.

You won't hurt me or anything will you?

I wasn't exactly sure how I was supposed to take this, but after my tussle I was feeling a little fatigued, so I told her, albeit politely, to shut up, then put tape over her mouth, did my best to hog-tie her, and held my fingers over her nostrils long enough for her to lose consciousness. I took a look around the apartment. Nothing caught my eye until I was heading for the door. On a table in a corner was a box full of all shape and presumably variety of pinecones. I took one as a souvenir for Mr. Kindt.

Lupe appeared not to have moved from the open doorway, although she now seemed agitated and was even wringing her hands. After a moment, I could hear a soft snoring coming out of the room behind her. I must have been disoriented, because I was suddenly overwhelmed by the feeling that all of New York, like some horrible dark spider, had crawled into the apartment behind Lupe to sleep and shouldn't, at all costs, be woken.

Bye, Lupe, I whispered.

A couple of gray cats had appeared and were sitting pressed up against her light-blue slippers.

Oftentimes, after I'd completed a job, I would go over to Mr. Kindt's and tell him about my evening. He liked hearing about what he called my escapades, and took particular interest in the ones that had a more openly theatrical aspect, like the job involving a rooftop terrace overlooking Tompkins Square, a black chair sitting on a red blanket, and poison dripped into an old guy's ear. He also took considerable pleasure in hearing about the simpler ones, including the murder of an older woman by following her into her apartment and smashing an ax into her head. Maybe not surprisingly, a considerable number of people were interested in death by falling, or smoke inhalation or sudden impact, and Mr. Kindt was always very interested to hear about how they had been accommodated.

Sometimes during these conversations, Tulip was present, and I have to say I tended to lay things on a little thick when she was there. Since our conversation in the bar after her murder, I had had the impression that certain elemental operations in my body, like cell mitosis or proper oxygen conversion or general nutrient replacement and calorie conversion, got interrupted when those eyes of hers would light on me. I had the impression that she had undergone an attitudinal adjustment toward me since the night of the second trial run, and, though it's a little embarrassing to admit, it was hard not to keep hearing her say, you're pretty too. Of course it's important not to overstate this perceived shift in circumstances. It's not like Tulip was suddenly falling all over me—hardly. Where before, a disinterested "whatever" might have come close to describing her attitude toward me, there now emanated some glimmer of maybe, just maybe, more than moderate interest from her direction when I would show up at Mr. Kindt's and start talking.

So of course I talked.

This talking, when it strayed from description of accomplished fake murder or of fake murder slated to be accomplished, was admittedly not much, but neither Mr. Kindt nor Tulip seemed greatly inclined to interrupt me. It was in this way that I came to discuss—with a level of bitterness that I only afterward and only vaguely wondered at— my unhappy early years in the city, the endless days spent working as a messenger in the basement at Forty-second and First, my dismissal, the brief and pleasant spell on severance and then unemployment, one or two incidents, my job shifting garbage and objects at the little antique shop on Second, my first attempted theft and its embarrassing result, a stint as a freelance writer for a weekly paper, the dismal try at a pulp novel, a Parisianesque girlfriend, several related episodes, including being dragged to poetry events at St.

Mark's Church and the KGB Bar, my general distrust of these events, where people either moved too much when they read or too little, the strange excitement of all the references to long-dead poets, the episode with my poor little cat, the Parisianesque girlfriend's abrupt and not unviolent and indeed heartbreaking departure from my life, my inability to make rent, certain family problems to do with my aunt, renewed attempts at theft, sketchy business opportunities, life on the streets, time in the hospital, where I was treated for my injuries, forcibly detoxed, given an opportunity to fill my pockets with some saleable pharmaceuticals, then discharged—in short, the whole sad story until Tulip walked up to me at a party, etc. Both Tulip and Mr. Kindt seemed sympathetic during my ramblings on this and other not especially related subjects, and at one juncture, when I was having an especially hard time describing something unpleasant that had occurred one night not too far from my old apartment, they told me to come sit between them on the couch.

You're past that and on to other things now, Henry, Mr. Kindt said.

Yes, Tulip said.

Anyway, generally speaking, they were both nice to me during these episodes. Mr. Kindt would say a few comforting words then gently steer me back to the subject of my escapades, and Tulip didn't get up and walk out of the room whenever I started talking, like she would have before. So it was all pretty agreeable.

Incidentally, I offer (or let stand) the above-mentioned biographical details, merely pointed to as they are, only to provide further context for my subsequent actions—to acknowledge, in a sense, that I had started my sad-sack downward slide long before Mr. Kindt, Tulip, Cornelius, and his posse entered my life, and that what was to happen very soon afterward, had as much to do with my own shortcomings—by that I mean my own idiocy—as with any particular external forces. Sure, there were machinations being conducted around me, but the truth is I had plenty of warning. To take one instance, the day of what I called the pinecone murder, in fact, Anthony appeared out of nowhere as I was heading over to Mr. Kindt's, grabbed my arm, and told me that he had been hearing things and that if I was smart I would put as much distance between myself and Mr. Kindt et al as I could. Instead of asking him why, what he'd been hearing, etc., what I did—and you will see that no matter how many questions I did actually ask I was to repeat the essence of this gesture several times in the days to come—was hold up the pinecone and say, Nice, huh?

TWENTY

There are two New Yorks. One of them is the one you go out into every day and every day it smacks you in the face and maybe you laugh a little and the people walk down the street and trucks blow their horns and you are happy or you are not, but your heart is beating. Your heart is beating as you walk, say, through a steady drizzle, your beat-up umbrella bumping other beat-up umbrellas, muttering excuse me, skirting small, dirty puddles and drifts of dark sediment, stepping out of the way of the young woman or young man on a cell phone who didn't see you coming, didn't notice you had stepped out of the way, didn't give a shit, didn't hear you say, because of this, fuck you, saying fuck you with your heart beating faster, feeling pretty good about saying fuck you, suddenly maybe feeling good about the drizzle, about the brilliant beads of water on the cabs going too fast down Prince, on the delicate ends of the oak branches as you cross Elizabeth, on the chain-link mesh as you move along the street. Your heart beats fast then slow then fast again as you cross Lafayette, the rainy vista extending all the way to Astor Place, then move across the shiny remnants of cobbles as you negotiate Crosby, the old, converted factory buildings surrounding you until you hit Broadway, where you can see up and down the shop-infested lower spine of New York, and you stop for a time and think about verticality, then compromised verticality, then rubble, about steaming ruins, about vanished buildings, and wonder where you're going, though not why. With money in your pocket and no place to be, why is not a question you are obliged to ask yourself as you start up again, a location in mind now, up Broadway past Houston then across Third, back to the East Village—home. There isn't any why as you wait at the light to cross Bowery, as you flip off a bike messenger who takes a puddle hard and sprays you with it, as you walk fast, in familiar territory again, as you stop in a bar and have a Cape Cod, as you smile a little but talk to no one, as you light a cigarette and close your eyes and lean back in your booth. For a short time then you subtract yourself from the proceedings, leave the cabs and chain link and cell phones outside, and, thinking of steam and rubble, drift. Down dark, windswept hallways, across empty public spaces, past vanished water-tasting stations and stopped-up springs, along oily waterways littered with rusting barges and sleeping gulls, down abandoned subway tunnels and the sparking guts of disused power stations: into the second New York. The one in which a heartbeat is at best a temporary anomaly, a troubling aftershock, an instance of unanswerable déjà vu. Which is much bigger than the first, and is for the most part, in your current condition, inaccessible to you, you think, although sometimes, like sitting in the bar drifting, or lying on your bed surrounded by lights and strangers, you can catch a glimpse.

You have caught glimpses at other times. Once was in a puddle on the asphalt one clear night after a long rain. You were walking along First Avenue, right above Forty-second, and had just gotten smacked by the flower truck, and you were on your hands and knees leaning over and there it was, or there you were, in those vast lands of the other city, the other New York, pale and scary, but not for long. Another time, earlier, you got a better look. This is how you know how big it is. This was when you still lived on the Lower East Side, not too far from the apartment you were about to lose, and you were getting the shit beaten out of you for having impolitely refused someone with bulging arm muscles and a toothpick in the corner of his mouth a sip of your Coke. Beaten so bad you had broken bones in your face and suffered partial memory loss and could only suppose what had happened after you had said, fuck no. So suppose you did. He had left you there with a screw-driver (fortunately only its butt was used) lying by your face—this became, in your imaginings: shot you up with a gat; chopped your shit with an ax; curbed you; stuck a grenade in your mouth; propped you up against a wall and smashed the back of a Buick into you; carried you up on top of one of the tenements and dropped you; cut your throat; poured gas on you and lit it; dragged you behind a lowrider; did something with a corkscrew; did something with a bat. You actually—and here your memory is unim-paired—spoke to yourself this time. You said to yourself, O.K., fine, all right, that's it, good-bye now, time to vanish, let's cruise. And you did. You left and wandered both alone and in company, walked arm in arm with yourself and with a couple million others, up and down the windy, gleaming streets of the necropolis, New York number two.

Little windows that opened onto this New York number two were of course omnipresent in the ward. Some days, when I didn't have a job to pull and I had gotten tired of reading or watching TV or waiting to see whether Dr. Tulp would stop by, I would grab Mr. Kindt and we would go take a look at people who, so it seemed, were dying. Mr. Kindt, who in this way was still the same old Mr. Kindt, despite the shift in our relationship, very much liked my theory of the two New Yorks, which he calculated became a dizzying sixteen million New Yorks if there was one of each for each New Yorker. I told him I wasn't sure if there was, in fact, a complementary New York for each of its inhabitants, or if it was just the pair of them, one size fits all and everyone on fucking top of each other in both. He said that either way, because he had no desire to leave New York under any circumstances, he found the concept of being ravished from one New York into another extremely comforting and it was never any trouble to get him to come along to look at people preparing to make the move. Sometimes, he was the one who suggested we go down and talk to the terminal cases on the second floor or prowl around in the critical wards, where, though this didn't matter when Mr. Kindt was with me, we weren't supposed to be. In fact, the duty nurses just looked at us without much interest and let us pass.

Certain arrangements have been made, Henry, not to worry, he said once when I wondered aloud about this.

So have certain arrangements been made for when I go closet shopping for resaleable items? I asked.

No, Henry, only so many arrangements of this sort are possible. On those occasions you will be on your own.

After we had returned—from talking, say, to a ninety-seven-year-old woman with a remarkably malignant skin cancer who had laughed out loud at the prospect of, as she put it, moving along, or from standing in the doorway of the burn unit and listening to the rise and fall of the respirators—we would sit together in one of our rooms and smoke and I would talk about the other New York and he would talk about the other Leiden and the other Amsterdam and the other Delft.

The one contains the other, I said.

The larger the smaller, or is it the other way around?

I don't know.

It is nevertheless a lovely notion, he said. All cities must be wrapped in a similar doubling embrace.

And all people, I said.

Yes, Henry, of course, we are all of us wrapped in the darkened shadows of our afterselves.

Which is where I would sit after Mr. Kindt left and I was alone again—with my shadow wrapped tightly around me, my robe and hands stinking of cigar smoke. I would sit and think about what we had both said and what we had seen earlier as we walked around. I would think about the other New York, with its long pulsing tunnels and skyscrapers made of helium and rods of light, or about the other Amsterdam, with its silver canals and velvet walls and tiny diamond bells.

One night after I had spent some time thinking I tried to pay a permanent visit to New York number two, but it didn't work. Despite what I thought was a pretty good effort. I didn't go anywhere.

I explained afterward to Dr. Tulp about the shadow surrounding me and also, for that matter, her.

You're Dutch, I said. You could probably go to some Dutch town. Eat good cheese. Paddle down the canals.

I'm not Dutch, Henry, Dr. Tulp said. And this idea of yours is stupid.

She ordered another adjustment to my meds and gave instructions that I wasn't to receive any visitors, instructions that, at least in the case of Mr. Kindt, weren't followed. He came the very first night carrying a cracker with a little bit of herring on it and said, eat, Henry, eat something and you will feel better.

It's the blue devil, I said.

It's too much talk and thinking about the great black yonder, Mr. Kindt said.

I meant you, you're the blue devil, I said.

Ah, yes.

The blue devil and the fish. Did I ever tell you about my dream where you were a fish, a herring in a black hat and hunting cape?

Mr. Kindt looked at me. He smiled. That's a funny dream, Henry, he said. When did you dream that?

When did you swim the length of Lake Otsego?

I don't follow.

Don't you?

I'm your friend, Henry. Your best friend. It's me. Aris.

That's a nice name, very nice. How did you come by it?

Mr. Kindt's smile, which had been holding steady, became its reverse.

I'm afraid of a sudden I find you a touch disagreeable, my boy, he said.

Well, you can bet you're not the first person to feel that way. Usually it's more than a touch. Can you even swim?

You should get back on your feet, Henry, he said, get some exercise, stop thinking so much, do that job.

I asked a question. How about an answer? I repeat, can you swim?

No. I can't. I never learned. Why are you asking me these questions?

I told him the truth, which was that I didn't know. They had just come to me. Had seemed important. Especially in the context of the shift that had occurred in our relationship.

Well, no doubt they are important. But now how about that job?

"That job" was related to some ampoules of pharmaceutical speed that Mr. Kindt had arranged for me to acquire. They were six hallways, two elevators, and a picked lock away.

I don't think I want to do it this time, Mr. Kindt, I said.

Ah, but you must, Henry. We must. After all, the window of opportunity is fast closing. And there are individuals involved who might turn their attention elsewhere if the desired items are not expeditiously secured.

Why can't you do it, you were a thief once, right?

A very long time ago I was a very bad thief.

So?

Mr. Kindt, who had been pacing back and forth, stopped and pointed his cracker at me.

In addition to being disagreeable, you seem, Henry, if perhaps you won't mind my saying so, somewhat less than grateful at the opportunity, the very bright conduit of possibility, that's been presented to you. I don't know what all this is about my name and swimming, but I am speaking of business, of transaction, and, more important, of obligation.

I didn't say anything. The unpleasant look I had seen in the hallway when he had broached the subject of stepping in for Job was back with a vengeance, and I didn't like the look of it at all. But I felt tired and my head hurt. And I was sad that things, which I thought had gone back to the way they were, definitely seemed to have transformed.

Please go away, I said.

Mr. Kindt stood there, indecisive, as if he wanted to keep haranguing me or maybe cut my throat, but then, although the hard look that had come into his eyes didn't entirely leave, it did soften, and his jaw relaxed, and he said, all right, my boy, yes, I can see you are tired, we'll talk later.

He came toward me with his herring-laden cracker, but I shook my head. He shrugged, put it into his mouth, and turned toward the door.

TWENTY-ONE

It was Tulip who told me who my next victim would be. It was near the end of a long night that started with a pleasant dinner at Mr. Kindt's apartment. There were no special guests that evening—just me and Tulip—and I had already, so to speak, killed (the accountant I had chloroformed and relieved of his documents) and talked about it, meaning I had nothing better to do after dinner than go back to The Fidelity and mutter to myself, the way my aunt used to do, and/or chew on the walls. So when Mr. Kindt, who for some time, under the guise of telling us about one of his early jobs in Cooperstown, had been holding forth on the subject of weaving and about the melancholy from which, as it is well-known, weavers have a tendency to suffer, all of a sudden said, wouldn't it be lovely if the two of you spent some time together, perhaps this very night, after dinner, I very quickly said, yes.

Not that, under any circumstances, I would have said no.

What do you think, Tulip? said Mr. Kindt.

Why not? Tulip said.

Then it's settled. Straight after dinner. Or after dinner and a game. Actually, let's start the game right now, while we finish. That way the two of you can depart all the more quickly.

The sooner the better as far as I was concerned, and Tulip was agreeable, so I went to get the game board. There wasn't any reason to ask which game Mr. Kindt wanted to play. There was only one in the apartment—Operation—and we played it frequently. Tulip had brought it home with her one evening early in the fall and when Mr. Kindt had seen what it was he had clapped his hands and squealed with delight. Operation, for those of you who missed out, is a game where the playing board is a man's body. The point is to remove the bones and organs without hurting the guy too much. You can tell you are hurting him when, in trying to remove one of the bones or organs from its narrow metal receptacle with a pair of metal tweezers, you touch the side and a buzzer goes off and the guy's big red nose lights up. The bones and organs have names like *bread basket, broken heart,* etc. It's fairly asinine. When we would play and the buzzer would go off, Mr. Kindt would giggle. The more the buzzer went off and the guy's nose lit up, the more Mr. Kindt would giggle. Tulip, with those long deft fingers, was the best at it and usually ended up with most of the organs. Mr. Kindt was easily the worst.

It was clear, in fact, that the whole thing for him was about the buzzer and the nose and making himself giggle.

Anyway, asinine or not, we started playing and pretty soon were all laughing in between bites of boiled vegetables and beef. I tried and failed three times to get the bread basket and Tulip tried and, surprisingly, failed to get the broken heart. Mr. Kindt said Tulip should keep trying to get the heart, and when she did on the next turn he clapped, whistled, pushed his chair back from the table, and did a little dance that concluded with the removal of his shirt.

Wow, I said.

Impressive, isn't it, Tulip said.

Mr. Kindt's chest, bare apart from the wires attached to it the last time I had seen it, was now speckled with tattoos.

At his suggestion, I inspected them and while I did so he pointed at the game board and then at his own chest, stomach, and lungs, and I concluded that, yes, they had been very skillfully (or, as Mr. Kindt put it, "very charmingly") done.

Tulip's work, said Mr. Kindt.

I gathered, I said.

All the body parts along with their receptacles from the board had been tattooed onto Mr. Kindt's torso.

My legs too, said Mr. Kindt. He said he had a bright red nose he could put on if I wanted to get the whole picture, the entire ensemble, but I said I thought I had the whole picture and that it was pretty cool.

Do you truly think it is cool? said Mr. Kindt.

Yes, I do, I said.

I am glad, my boy, I am very glad. Perhaps one of these evenings the two of you could use me as the board.

Mr. Kindt giggled.

I'd like to get a tattoo, I said.

I'll give you one tonight, Tulip said.

We ate and played a little more and talked about this and that. Mr. Kindt, who had calmed down, though he hadn't put his shirt back on, said he still felt like talking and asked if we wouldn't, after all, mind postponing our departure a touch longer. We said that we wouldn't, of course, and that he should talk as much as he wanted to, so he did. He started with combustion, positing it as the hidden principle behind nearly all human endeavor, which led to a discussion of furnaces and iron factories and forest fires. He then related an interesting anecdote about a certain saint, Sebold, who was ascribed the extravagance of having made icicles burn, citing this as an example of the extremes to which we, as a species, will go to separate ourselves from cold and from things lurking and from dark.

Incidentally, when it is my own time, he said, I should like to be cremated, not buried. The prospect of slowly dissolving beneath the cold, so to speak, clay strikes me as more than mildly alarming. Cremation is very nearly as ancient a farewell ritual as burial and is infinitely brighter. If you think of it, you might throw some cedar wood or other aromatic onto the pyre.

Mr. Kindt then spoke a little about Cornelius and about the success of his business and about the important role I had played in ensuring that success. My excellent work that very evening with the accountant—its extraordinary authenticity—was a prime example.

I must confess that I have been very lucky in my business dealings, perhaps because I tend to endorse interesting projects like this one, he said. I do not know how much longer the market for a service like Cornelius's will be there, but it has already paid, and handsomely, for itself. Mr. Kindt then noted the positive impact the service had had on my life. Not least because I had been presented with an opportunity and had grabbed it. The opportunity had come out of the blue and I had at first gotten involved out of friendship, but in his opinion that in no way undercut the significance of the gesture.

It is simply a matter of stepping forward, he said. A moment arrives and we step forward. Of course there is circumstance but the circumstance is ultimately unimportant. It is the stepping-forward that matters. Just a step and we are there. Don't you think this is so, Henry?

I nodded slowly to show that I wasn't quite with him.

I'm simply speaking, dear boy, of assertion in its most elemental form. The organism, engaged in drifting, alters its course. It steps forward. What happens afterward is necessarily adjusted. I stepped forward on the shore of Lake Otsego one night many years ago.

You mean you swam forward.

Mr. Kindt laughed. Of course, he said. There was a moment and I slipped into it. The years, which were to unfurl otherwise, perhaps much less fruitfully, were obliged by my action that night to alter their trajectory.

And Cornelius's?

Yes, Cornelius's too. Cornelius was very helpful, in fact, in facilitating the execution of my move forward.

You mean he paid up after you won the bet?

Is that what you mean, Aris? said Tulip, who had been sitting quietly with her legs pulled up to her chest.

Mr. Kindt shook his head.

But he was there, I said.

Oh yes, he was there.

I asked Cornelius about it the other day and he said something about how nice your name was.

Ah? Well, it is a nice name, isn't it. Rich in consonants and the nimblest, most crystalline vowel. I have often wondered what my namesake thought of it.

Tell us about the first Aris Kindt, Tulip said.

There isn't terribly much to tell. He has been killed and is lying in the middle of his own misery.

Tulip and I followed Mr. Kindt's gaze across the room to the framed reproduction of Rembrandt's *The Anatomy Lesson*. The painting showed a dead guy being worked over by a doctor. A group of men looked on. There was light on the scene but the corpse's face was in shadow. Mr. Kindt stood up, walked across the room, and put his finger on the dead guy's chest.

That, he said, is the sad originator of my name. Well, officially he was named Adriaan Adriaanson. But his alias, his professional name, the one he was killed under, was Aris Kindt.

Your namesake is a dissection victim?

The namesake of my namesake, but yes.

What do you mean, "the namesake of my namesake"? You've said that before.

Yes, tell us, Aris, said Tulip.

Mr. Kindt did not tell us. Instead he raised an eyebrow, let it fall, and came back toward us.

I've had great occasion to think of him lately, of this unfortunate individual from whom I derive my name, this man who has been given a face by history, an anguished face cast into shadow, a false name that has blotted out the real one, a body whose tenure has been forcibly completed, a body that is being opened so that its interior functions, its revelatory organs, may be apprehended. Hence, I suppose, my interest in our little postprandial games.

He straightened himself up and looked down at his tattooed body.

It is no doubt inevitable that Cornelius's reentry into my life has brought my thoughts on the matter back to the fore.

I asked him what he meant. He didn't answer. He did say though that he fully respected what he described as the "recent trend" in his relationship with Cornelius and wanted us both to know that it was perfectly understandable.

Tulip then asked him if he would characterize his relationship with Cornelius as loving or as intricate.

Both, my dear, he said, plopping into his chair. After all, history and night and water and now both of you are involved. What do you say we move on to something else?

At this, Tulip said that she had seen the one-time bartender and second murderer, Anthony, and had had a couple of drinks with him.

He's glad to be out of it, she said. He thought we were all creepy.

Mr. Kindt said, oh well, you know, he does rather have a point. What has he found to do with himself?

He works as an orderly at one of the hospitals in midtown, said Tulip. Does things like administer shots and serve meals and give sponge baths.

I saw him too, I said. Not long ago. He told me I should think about getting out of the business and find some other friends.

Well, that's probably not the worst advice, but I do, ha, ha, hope you aren't thinking of taking it, which reminds me, Mr. Kindt said, then began talking again. At some point in this talking with Mr. Kindt, sitting there with his shirt still off, looking about as much like a crumpled game board as like his namesake, Tulip stood up, put her coat on, and said, let's go.

TWENTY-TWO

I made my first and only serious play for Dr. Tulp's affections not long after my latest distressing conversation with Mr. Kindt. I had the feeling, and I was not wrong, that things, if not coming to a head, were shifting into a terrain that would be murkier, more confusing, harder to effectively negotiate, so before one of her scheduled visits I threw off my hospital regalia, scrubbed myself at great length under an extra-hot shower, shaved carefully, then put on the only noninstitutional clothes I had—the ragged but clean three-piece vintage suit I had been wearing when I was brought in. I always used to like to apply a reasonable amount of thick pomade to my hair, and had managed to keep up this practice even when I was spending both nights and days on the streets, but there wasn't any available in the hospital, so I contented myself with pulling my wet hair back tight against my head and holding it there until it was more or less dry.

Establishing an agreeable ambience in any hospital room is a problem, and for a while I shoved and pulled various objects—like the bedclothes, the dirty linen hamper, the curtains, the TV—this way and that, then experimented with various arrangements of the room's key infrastructure—the bed, the side table, and the chair. When I was satisfied with the configuration, I made a quick trip around the ward and gleaned two fairly fresh bouquets of flowers and half a dozen still somewhat buoyant green and gold balloons from a recently vacated room, and did a few things with them.

The effect, when I was finished, was interesting, if not impressive, which I thought would be likely to play well with Dr. Tulp. I was certainly hoping this would be the case when she considered me. I had lost a pretty good deal of weight by this point and my suit, which was already a little baggy, fell, let's say, differently than a suit should, and of course I didn't have any shoes, only my large white slippers. Also my skin had gone a little sallow during my stay, so that under the bright light in front of the bathroom mirror I had a kind of jaundice thing going. But doctors are trained to see past surfaces, to look at the greatest corporeal horrors and smile, or yawn, so I didn't have any trouble imagining that Dr. Tulp's gaze would cut right through the really only mildly deficient portions of my exterior aspect and appreciatively palpitate the softer, richer surfaces beneath. Well, that's what I was counting on. Just in case, I pulled the curtains closed and turned off all the lights except the one with the dimmer switch beside my bed, which I set nice and low. I then splashed a little alcohol on my cheeks, rubbed them with a dry bar of soap in hopes that some of the fragrance would stick, did the same with my wrists and ankles, then climbed onto the bed, crossed my arms and ankles, and set out to wait.

Unfortunately, I fell asleep. So that when Dr. Tulp did come in I greeted her first with a grunt then a disoriented shriek sparked by my perception, in the dim light, with the balloons bobbing in the middle distances and flowers and flower stalks strewn across the floor and various surfaces, that it was Mr. Kindt, not Dr. Tulp, who was moving, not through my room but instead some grotesque, aqueous grotto, toward me. I quickly recovered though, so that when she greeted me and said, what's going on in here, Henry? I was in a position to smile and invite her to come over and take a seat by the bed. Her response to this was to flip on the lights, press the call button, then chew out the nurse for letting me, in so many words, trash the room.

This definitely didn't look too good for my prospects, and I probably would have given up on them right then, but instead of instructing me and the nurse to start cleaning up, she told the nurse that would be all, waited until she had left the room, then turned the lights back off.

Do you want me to turn this dimmer up?

No, that's all right, she said. In fact, it's perfect in here.

Perfect, huh? I said.

Dr. Tulp batted at one of the balloons as she crossed the room to the chair. There was a balloon within my own reach so I batted at it. Our balloons drifted off in opposite directions for a few feet then went back to bobbing.

I once took part in a school rendition of *The Tempest*, said Dr. Tulp, as she sat down, leaned back a little in the chair, and crossed her long legs. We did a kind of flower thing like this for the cave. We also hung metallic streamers and blinking Christmas lights and pasted plastic jewels all over the place. When he saw it, the director said it looked like the interior of one of those Bangladeshi restaurants and wondered if we wanted to call for takeout.

I bet you played the wizard's daughter.

No, I played the wizard's slave.

Well, I would have liked to have seen that, Dr. Tulp. I said this with as much come-hither as my voice could muster. She didn't, so I tried something else.

I was in some plays in school.

Oh?

Do you want to hear about them?

Dr. Tulp looked thoughtfully at me. I took this to mean I should go ahead. I started to tell her about playing the donkey in the *Bremen Town Musicians*, but she cut me off.

No?

She shook her head. I have to admit this flummoxed me a little. I pulled my legs up and wrapped my hands around them. She leaned forward and put her elbows on her knees.

Did you do this for me, Henry? she said. Her pale white hand did a pretty little back dive as she said this. I imagined it back-diving and back-stroking across the room and out the window. I imagined my own hand following it, out into the air high above the streets.

Well, yeah, I said.

It's nice, she said. I mean it's awful and you look awful, especially in that old suit, but it's nice. The gesture, I mean. You may think I'm impervious to flattery but I'm not. In fact, I like it very much.

The hand that had been swimming reached out and touched a bit of sheet on the bed. A big smile lit my face.

Can I call you Nicola? I said.

I've scheduled you for surgery, she said.

What? What are you talking about? When? I said.

She leaned back, looked at her watch, looked at me, pressed the call button, and said, now.

TWENTY-THREE

The brief adventures of Henry and Tulip began in a little tattoo parlor on Orchard Street, where Tulip went to work on my chest, repeatedly jamming a needle into the strip of skin covering my heart.

What is it? I asked.

You can look later, she said. It's just something simple. A souvenir. The irritation will go away soon.

She brought me over a glass of water and a couple of Tylenol and told me to take them. I did so, then wiped my mouth, then told her I'd had a dream about this place, only it had been transformed into a kind of operating room and we were all swimming around and she was cutting Mr. Kindt to pieces. She was smiling and cutting into him and talking about it and pretty soon we all came over and watched. By the end we were in a kind of semicircle around the operating slab while she cut and tugged.

Sound familiar? I said as I put my shirt back on.

How funny, she said.

Yes, I said. Did you bring Anthony here after your drinks?

Be nice, she said.

Then we went to Grand Central.

Grand Central Station was recently renovated. Renovation meaning that a lot of expensive shops have been added, and that you can really truly and profitably look up at the ceiling in the central concourse, which has reclaimed its brass and marble heritage, and learn a thing or two about the zodiac, because now it has been cleaned.

Scorpio, said Tulip, looking up at the ceiling, how about you?

I said what I was, and Tulip said, Mr. Kindt too, and I said, speaking of, any idea what was going on tonight?

What do you mean?

You know: the namesake of the namesake and the namesake is a corpse with an alias and the recent trend in his relationship with Cornelius and the thing about stepping forward.

Tulip shrugged.

I looked at her.

She shrugged again.

So I said, O.K., now what?

Now we go.

What do you mean, go?

We're taking a little trip.

Right now?

Soon.

But first she wanted to show me something. We went down one of the two conjoining chandelier-lit slopes that mediate between the upper and lower levels of the station and stopped under a central walkway, near enough to the Oyster Bar that I thought that was where we were going. Instead, Tulip told me to go stand over in one of the corners of the intersection made by the two slopes and the passage leading down from the restaurant.

Turn around and put your face against the wall, she said.

Seriously? I said.

It's clean. Or clean enough.

I leaned forward. The tile, where I touched it, was cool against my forehead, which was pleasant, as thinking about my dream and Mr. Kindt and Rembrandt et al had gotten me a little heated. I pressed my forehead harder against the tile, took a deep breath, then pulled away and looked over my shoulder. Tulip was more or less doing the same thing in the opposite corner, looking very good doing it. Then she was talking to me.

Henry, she said.

Her voice seemed to be coming out of the piece of tile in front of my face.

Nice, I said.

How's your chest?

It hurts.

That's normal.

What's the tattoo?

Like I said, it's a little keepsake.

Something to remember you by?

That's right.

Are you going somewhere?

We're going somewhere.

Where?

We're leaving, getting out.

Out of New York?

You interested?

Very. I guess.

Good. But, Henry, promise me something.

Sure.

No more comments about Anthony, all right? That's boring. You have to give it a rest. Mind your own business.

O.K., you're right, sorry, I said.

Anyway, we are creepy, Henry. Anthony has a point.

I'm creepy?

But she didn't answer, wasn't there anymore.

I found her a couple of minutes later standing by the information booth soaking up, she said, the train station atmosphere, something she had liked to do as a kid.

I wasn't quite done talking, I said.

So talk, she said.

But, beyond elaborating on the subject of creepiness, which suddenly seemed to me painfully self-evident and basically played out, or trying to dig a little more at the conversation we'd had at Mr. Kindt's, which seemed to be covered by the creepiness thing anyway, I didn't really have anything to say.

There were plenty of people going by and Tulip blabbed a little, in watered-down Mr. Kindt style, remarking, for example, on the patterns the people made striding across the regularly cleaned marble floors and going up and down the marble staircases and I said, uh huh.

Then it was time to catch the train we were apparently interested in, so we went downstairs to track 122, which was hot and crowded despite the late hour. There were a couple of conductors conferring at the top of the platform, wearing their tall blue hats and short-sleeve shirts, and the inside of the train was brightly lit, but cool and surprisingly quiet given the amount of activity. I thought then of that feeling you get on a train that is just leaving the station, going slowly, and all the heads in the car are rocking back and forth and the lights blink on and off and there is a strange calm. Thinking about this, I began to feel a little better and more hopeful.

This is very nice, I said.

Yes, it is, Tulip said.

Where's this train going? I didn't look.

No idea. It's the New Haven line. I think Portchester is one of the stops. Maybe Stamford.

So we're just going to see where it takes us?

She looked out the window at the gray platform, her face clearly reflected in the dirty glass.

Mr. Kindt wants you to murder him, she said.

Come again, I said.

There's a script.

I looked down at my hands. They looked in need of some scrubbing. I felt my face flushing, the heat coming back. Is that why we came out tonight, so you could tell me that? Was that the whole point?

It was Aris's idea. He wanted me to be the one to ask you.

Why?

Think about it.

I thought. Just then the conductor came over the intercom to announce the train's imminent departure. People kept coming in, taking their coats off, putting bags on the overhead racks, unfolding newspapers, opening books.

What kind of murder are we talking about? I said.

You'll have to ask Cornelius, he has the script now.

I'm asking you.

She didn't answer.

He wanted you to ask because it's part of the script.

Tulip nodded.

I would have figured he'd go for something more exotic. Something intricate or whatever.

His tastes are sometimes surprising. I mean, his favorite game *is* Operation.

He wants it to play like a B movie, something a little racy. His lovely young friend, who stands to gain in some significant way, persuades a creepy young ne'er-do-well down on his luck to bump him off. It's like a poor man's version of *The Postman Always Rings Twice*.

Tulip smiled. That ends badly, she said.

It certainly does.

And I wouldn't say you're down on your luck.

But you would say I'm creepy.

Yes, but not that you're a ne'er-do-well.

After she said this she leaned over and kissed me on the cheek.

Was that part of the scenario?

She didn't answer. Instead, she said, I am kind of lovely, aren't I?

She was. There was no doubt about it. There was no, in fact, getting around it, not for me.

Why not Cornelius or the knockout or the contortionists? I said. He could have gotten something cheap and thrilling out of them. Why me?

I don't know, she said. Because it turns out you're good. Because you got him excited with all those descriptions of murders. Because, clearly, he's eccentric. Because he's a rich guy from Cooperstown who likes to play, among other things, crime boss in the village.

Play crime boss?

I was kidding. Exaggerating for effect. It's just that by now he doesn't have to do anything. He's like a consultant. He does some things for some people. Other people do things for him.

People like Cornelius.

Tulip nodded.

O.K., and while we're at it, what about Cooperstown, where he made his big stake? What did he do besides supposedly weaving straw baskets before he took his famous swim? Before Cornelius helped him to "step forward," whatever that means.

What do you think it means?

I think it means something besides a swim and a bet happened that night. Am I close?

What do I know?

Considerably more than I do, I thought. Or should have.

He likes you, Henry. He wants a turn. Forget the other stuff. Forget Cooperstown. They've got issues. They've known each other for, what, a million years? It's their thing. Love and intricacy. Let's leave it at that.

Tulip gave me a little shove. I gave her a little shove back. By this time we were standing out on the platform and the train was pulling away. It moved slowly into the dark tunnel that would take it across the Bronx, out of the city, and into the lamp- and moonlit suburbs, where mysteries of another order abounded and people drank cocktails out of cut glass and swam, etc., only after the sun had set behind beautiful trees. For a moment, I had the feeling that I was still on the train as it snaked its way through the dark. As it seemed to me I sat there, head bobbing while the lights went on and off, Tulip's hand snaked down my arm, over my wrist, and her fingers curled tightly around my own. She squeezed, leaned close, bit my ear, and, reprising Cornelius's speech from dinner the first night, said, "If they dyed by violent hands, and were thrust into their Urnes, these bones become considerable."

I'm leading a strange fucking life here, I thought.

TWENTY-FOUR

After my surgery the ward seemed to grow enormous—so that when I left my room to stretch my legs the distances unfurling before me were dizzying—then tiny—so that the possibility of stretching my legs was rendered impossible by the robin-egg-sized dimensions that greeted me when I opened my door. This torquing of the space surrounding me, which I had no doubt whatsoever was self-imposed, fortunately ended almost as soon as it had begun, so that when, on my third try, I left my room to stretch my legs, everything had resumed its natural order. It had not, however, quite resumed its natural quality. By this I mean that while before the surgery everything my eyes had gazed upon had seemed relatively dull, dreary, lackluster, matte, etc., now as I walked around the corridors I encountered the kind of visual clarity that I had until then associated with the south of France or the Greek Islands, or the beach at Coney Island on one of those beautiful September days. Everything I looked at seemed to have been polished or resurfaced. When I looked at the microwave oven set into what had been a drab alcove in the drab visitor's lounge, for example, I had the feeling I was standing in an open quarry with a brilliant afternoon light behind me and that what I had before me was some fresh shape made of metals and minerals pulled straight out of the ground and shot through a replicator then scoured by robots with high-speed buffers. Anyway, that's the direction in which my thoughts tended as I took in the microwave, the marvelously vivid lime and mauve textures of the old couch by the window, the sharply delineated lines of the bits and pieces of detritus—fuzz, dirt, latex glove, a torn business card belonging to a real-estate photographer whose name and number were missing, etc.—scattered here and there across the floor.

Despite all this visual finery, and the exhilarating sensations I got by taking it in, however, I didn't feel at all well. In fact, I was forced to hold my side and hunch over a little as I maneuvered around the visitor's lounge to peer at this and that, so I was unprepared—and this unpreparedness gave me quite a shock, in fact forced me to fall over onto the gleaming couch—when Aunt Lulu, who had probably been there watching me all along, seemed to appear next to the refrigerator.

Aunt Lulu, I said.

My goodness and gracious, Henry, she said.

I just had surgery.

Well it certainly does look like you just had something. Surgery? How awful.

Aunt Lulu smiled. I couldn't quite believe it. A row of fresh clean choppers beamed out of her face at me.

You've got teeth, Aunt Lulu, I said.

I beg your pardon?

Your mouth—it's full of teeth.

Well of course it is. Listen to you. Why wouldn't it be?

I didn't answer, because I was taking in the rest of her. She had on a snug green polka-dot dress and green heels and was dangling a pocketbook with a gold-chain handle on her wrist. Her hair, which I had only ever seen more or less plastered to her head and dripping with grease, or in week-old worn-out curlers, was done up in a kind of bouffant, and her eyelashes were as long and curved and dark as some of the thoughts I'd been having.

You look different, Aunt Lulu, I said, hoping that the irony of the understatement would get through loud and clear. If it did, she didn't give any sign of it.

I heard you wanted to see me again, she said.

Who said that?

A kind of horrifying little pouty expression appeared on her face then vanished.

Don't you want to see me? she said.

No, I thought. Then I thought of standing up, started to, then decided I'd better wait until I had rested a little. Not least because I didn't want Aunt fucking Lulu with her bouffant hair to see me groan and fail.

I'm always happy to see you, Aunt Lulu, I said. Have you met Dr. Tulp yet? She's the one who just operated on me. They used a local anesthetic. It didn't work very well, didn't quite do the trick. I told them that. Told them I could feel the scraping. That it felt like they were using a rusty straightedge to shave my heart.

Is she in charge here, Henry?

I don't know. You look different to me, Aunt Lulu. You've done something with your hair. You've got a clean dress on. You look like you've slimmed up. It's bright in here. And hot. Don't you think it's hot? Do you want to speak in tongues?

I stuck my tongue out and tried to say a few things.

Henry, she said. She waved her hand back and forth a

couple of times through the sparkling air then flipped it over, snapped her fingers to her palm, and inspected her long green nails. In the brilliant light, the tips of her fingers looked like emeralds under a halogen bulb. When, satisfied with the first hand, she switched to the other, my eyes moved with hers.

I was staring at her fingernails when she said, ah, there you are.

At first I assumed she had said this to me, that she had decided that the best way to remedy the not-promising interaction we had going was to pretend that, rather than sitting motionless on the couch, sort of hunching over my side and staring at her hands, I had just walked into the room. I was no more sure what to make of this than I was of how she looked and sounded, so I just kept staring at her hands. But she wasn't talking to me at all.

Hello, Lulu, Mr. Kindt said.

Aris, I've just been chatting with Henry, she said.

Mr. Kindt came around the couch, patted me on the knee, then stood on tiptoe and kissed Aunt Lulu on both cheeks. They smiled at each other, then Mr. Kindt turned so that they both were facing me. He too was preternaturally lit, and even though I found myself being swept by a rising surge of nausea—which I had been told to expect following my surgery, but that I attributed to the sight of Mr. Kindt and Aunt Lulu standing together—it's also true that the combination of her green nails and his blue eyes, which reminded me of the burning-blue, backlit orbs haunting the heads of the spice-eating desert dwellers in David Lynch's film version of *Dune,* was mesmerizing.

We met in the hallway as I was leaving last time, Aunt Lulu said.

Mr. Kindt nodded. I thought I would take your aunt on a tour of the ward today, Henry, show her some of the sites, get her acquainted with our little stomping ground.

But then I'll come back, Aunt Lulu said. After all, I did come to talk to *you*, Henry.

What on earth, Aunt Lulu, could we possibly have to talk about? I wanted to ask. The majority of me, including my vocal apparatus, however, seemed to want only to sit there, unmoving, unresponsive, legs slightly spread, hands in my lap.

Likely sensing that I wasn't up for an active discussion anymore, Aunt Lulu said, you are tired, nephew. Your friend Aris here can entertain me. We'll walk around and then I'll come back and see you.

Her nails shone even more brightly as she said this, and her brown eyes seemed to have caught some of the fire in Mr. Kindt's.

I want to discuss a thing or two with you, Henry, she said. I want to talk to you about some things, including the way I understand that you have been portraying me to the good people here, discussing my appearance and comportment as if we didn't all have good and bad days. I want to talk about that in some depth, Henry.

She took Mr. Kindt's arm, and they stepped forward so that they were only a foot or so away from my kneecaps.

I thought I'd show her the garden, Mr. Kindt said. I haven't been out there today. Perhaps we'll see some birds. Do you smoke, my dear?

Oh yes, I love a good smoke, Aris, she said. Let's go and do just what you propose—let's see the ward and smoke in the garden and you can show me the birds if they are around. You can introduce me to the various people here, including Dr. Tulp, who I understand is Henry's primary care physician. Especially Dr. Tulp, who I trust can give me a fair and accurate accounting of my nephew's condition. And then I want to come back and speak directly to him. I want to speak to him about his portrayal of others and about his character. I want to see what he has to say about that. I want to talk to my nephew and pick his brain a little on some of these subjects and give him the opportunity to pick mine.

Then I want to sit with him, very close to him if he still isn't feeling well, and talk to him about the circumstances of my death. I'd like to ask him to describe it, to tell me what it looked like from where he was standing. He was right there, Aris. Right there in the doorway.

Ah, said Mr. Kindt.

And he didn't move a muscle, so I imagine he had a very clear view of what happened. He was a very interesting boy, Aris, always full of opinions and never hesitant to share them. I'd like to hear what he has to say. There is a great deal—isn't there, Henry?—to discuss. We can put our heads together and talk about the past and our relationship and about the way—let's call it abrupt, my god yes it was abrupt—that Henry here helped cut it off. Sound good?

Sounds brilliant, Lulu, Mr. Kindt said.

Both of them beamed at me.

Toodles, Aunt Lulu said, grazing my scalp with her nails as they went past.

Oh fuck, I said.

All the wonderful light seemed like it might start scorching the room.

TWENTY-FIVE

The rising sun was dribbling rivulets of light into the troughs of the crosstown streets when I left the little room behind the tattoo parlor on Orchard and made my way back to The Fidelity. Mr. Mancini was asleep with his head in his arms on the front desk when I came in, which was a shame because I was in the mood to crow a little about my night. In fact, I was so eager to let Mr. Mancini know what I had gotten myself up to after leaving Grand Central—without providing details of course—in Tulip's arms as we lay on the AeroBed on the floor in the corner next to the low shelf with the burning ylang-ylang candle, and, spurred on by contextually vast expanses of exposed skin and numerous murderous propositions, created friction, that I stood a minute in front of him, doing a little bit of a shuffle and spin dance on the cracked tiles of the entryway and staring at the swirly roots of the thick dark hair covering the top of his cinder-block-sized head. However, when thoughts of crowing a little—who's the shitface now that I scored with Tulip?—gave way to— wouldn't it be nice to maybe knock this guy on his ugly egg with a phone book and see if he wakes up smiling?—I decided I should probably skip the Mr. Mancini interlude, which would just end badly anyway, and go up to my room.

I woke coughing a few hours later. The air had been all but replaced by a noxious mix of tar, motor oil, and old

chewing gum, which meant that one of the hot dog vendors who kept his cart in the storefront attached to The
Fidelity had forgotten to extinguish his coals, and the fumes
had come up the air shaft. Since the guy who leased to the
hot dog vendors was Mr. Mancini's brother-in-law, the only
thing to do about it was get dressed, listen to a wide-awake
Mr. Mancini snarl preemptive disclaimers through the nasty
smile that was already, even at 8:30 in the morning, plastered onto his face, and get out.

So I hit the streets a little more blearily than I might have
liked, and this bleariness contributed, I have very little
doubt, to the gradual nosedive my spirits took over the
course of the morning. It wasn't, at least not at first, that I
no longer felt pretty fabulous about my late evening exer-
tions with Tulip: I did. It's just that part of my pleasure in
contemplating the proceedings on Tulip's AeroBed, proceedings that had lasted beyond any reasonable expectation, was
mitigated by a sense of disbelief that gained ground as I
sipped coffee on the bench outside Porto Rico on St. Mark's
Place, chewed a bagel I got on B, and read part of a
Wolverine comic book I retrieved from a trash can on
Seventh, and that was confirmed when I stood in front of a
mirror in the men's room in a café on Third and A.

Wait a minute, uck, there is no way Tulip did that voluntarily, is what I thought.

Now, it wasn't as if I hadn't made an effort since I had
gotten into murders, despite the challenges presented by living at a dump like The Fidelity, to keep myself more or less
presentable and to acquire some new clothing. In fact, at
that very moment, I had on my favorite green rooster T-
shirt, a pair of fairly clean, nicely rumpled linen pants, and

some acceptable leather on my feet. But the truth was, even if it was possible that I was heading toward brighter days and a better look, I hadn't gotten there yet. Not even close. I tried to imagine lasciviously sidling up to myself, failed, and had to splash water on my face. Fortunately, splashing water on my face made me think of Mr. Kindt and thinking of him, especially in this context, helped. Tulip did, after all, spend a tremendous amount of time around our benefactor, who, despite the odd feature or two, was, let's face it, despite those special aspects, no gorgeous picture himself. I might, I thought, actually be just exactly what the doctor ordered for Tulip, just the perfect soup, the loveliest piece of pickled fish, the most extraordinary, because so unusually textured, chunk of baguette. I had, after all, enjoyed the company of a girlfriend who had loved me, or put up with me, for a very long time, and she had been far from some kind of kook or tasteless slouch. True, I had been in much better shape in those days, at least until that period at the end when it all collapsed, when it all came crashing down on me. Until that time I had without a doubt been what she once referred to, while we ate steak frites—my treat—at Belmondo, a "most satisfactory companion," but still.

There were other things from the previous night to think about as I walked around that morning, little things— to do with Cornelius, and Mr. Kindt, and the nature of Tulip's relationship to them—that, as you will see when I discuss the night of the murder later on, further problematized this question of the authenticity of Tulip's regard for my physical person, and I did kick them around some, but mostly I considered, and mostly, in the end, fought off, doubts of a principally aesthetic nature.

Then I got hungry. The morning had closed up shop so I opted for a slice. Two Boots was, happily, just across the street when my stomach started grumbling. I sidestepped between a couple of parked Toyotas, let a few cabs shark their way by, and made for its welcoming doors.

Two Boots on Avenue A is one of those terrific spots that purists—partisans of Ray's this and Ray's that—turn their noses up at, but after too many years of getting burnt by the too-often mediocre results of tradition I had come to love it. At Two Boots, you can have your so-called plain slice with just the right amount of marinara and not too much cheese, or you can put your money down, as I like to, on one of the many slices with unusual names: The Night Tripper, Mel Cooley, Mr. Pink, Mrs. Peel, Big Maybelle, and so on. I had in mind a slice of Bayou Beast (shrimp, crawfish, andouille, jalapeño, and mozzarella), one of The Newman (Soppressata, sweet Italian sausage, ricotta, and mozzarella), a few shakes each of Parmesan, oregano, and hot pepper, a large, well-iced fountain Diet Pepsi, and a seat at the back booth by the john. I saw all of this as I crossed Avenue A, then felt and smelled and tasted it—for some reason the icy imagined Diet Pepsi coming up under my top lip as I sipped between imagined bites was particularly vivid—and, in short, worked myself into the kind of minor frenzy I began experiencing during my rougher days in the city whenever low blood sugar or whatever had kicked in and, money in pocket, I was minutes away from food.

Gratification was put off by a beleaguered-looking couple making the classic big production of getting out the front door with a stroller. I sort of theatrically stepped aside and swept my arm out to let them know that I wouldn't be interfering, in any way whatsoever, with their forward baby-propelling propagation, and they both said thanks so simultaneously that I couldn't help blurting "jinx." This made the woman laugh and the guy smile. The baby, who had a lot of blond hair for such a shrimpy customer, let out a squawk, and they were off.

I only mention this because as I stood at the counter surveying the Pinks and Beasts and Big Maybelles, thinking that they ought to add a Mr. Kindt to their lineup, a kind of prestige slice with cracker crumbs and pickled herring on a white pie, two people said "I got it" at the same time, and a third voice, older, gravelly, accented, familiar, said "jinx." Given that I never say "jinx" and that I haven't heard it said in years, I turned to see who had spoken. But just then my order was taken and, because I occasionally frequented Two Boots and knew some of the guys there, a little chitchat was indicated, and by the time my slices were up and I had taken a spot not in the back, but in one of the big booths on Avenue A, the "jinx" thing had slipped my mind. It came back to me though when the two "I got it" guys burst into conversation in the booth behind me about some book one of them was reading called *Stranger Things Happen*. Deep into the baked aquatic mysteries of my first bite of Bayou Beast, I half expected—in that bleary mind-fried way—the one who was reading it to start talking about Mr. Kindt or maybe the contortionists. Instead he went into a detailed description of a story about a ghost who can't remember his name, which elicited a few too many guffaws from his companion for me to relax and enjoy my slices, so I moved to the table by the front door where, even though you have to stand and the foot traffic is pretty steady, the experience would be relatively untainted by over-easy joke-truffled book talk.

As I was standing there an old guy wearing a fedora and a wife beater came over with a slice of Mel Cooley, slapped a Miller down on the table, and, in that vaguely familiar voice, asked me to slide over the oregano.

Jinx, I said.

He looked blankly at me for a second then laughed.

This time of the day you can usually count on eating and maybe conversing in some peace here but not today, no sir, they're even talking at the same time as each other, he said.

Amen, I said.

Mel the Hat, he said.

It took me a moment to realize I had just been told what I should call him. I nodded and said my own name.

I used to know a Henry, years back. We used to do business together. Small stuff. Good times. You ever do any business?

He looked at me with the kind of misty gray eyes that only the very old or very beautiful have. I wasn't sure about the latter, but there was no doubt about the former. I figured he had to have at least fifteen years on Mr. Kindt. Maybe twenty.

No comment, I said.

He clapped his hands, let out a laugh, and said, I knew it. I could tell. I could have told you, this guy is doing business.

I took a sip of my drink. He lifted his Mel Cooley and sunk what had to be false teeth into a clot of ricotta and roasted pepper. His voice, which was high-pitched and Dominican-inflected, definitely sounded like something I had rattling around somewhere in my head.

I'm sorry, no offense, but what I said was, no comment.

Sure, he said. And much better that way too. You have to forgive me—I'm out now. I'm done. They got a box paid up and waiting for me up at Plascencia's and some green space to go with it and all my scores are settled. I spot individuals and sometimes I talk to them. I'm too old now to matter, so generally they don't care. I don't usually ask specific questions. But I do got one for you.

I raised my eyebrow, bit into some Italian sausage, and nodded.

How's your back?

My back? I said through the flecks of demolished crust, cayenne, and oregano scattered around my mouth like delicious storm debris.

You got any issues? Bad knees? You look pretty good.

The tassel of his fedora kept flipping back and forth as he spoke. He seemed to be hopping from leg to leg. He was old but the engine wasn't sputtering yet. I said that my back and knees were fine.

He clapped his hands. I thought so. You look like you got highly functioning shoulders. You want to help me out?

I shrugged. I told him I was fairly busy. I asked him what he meant.

Just boxes, he said. My sister has some boxes up in the closet and she wants them down. I was thinking maybe you could come help me out.

We left via the video store attached to the pizza parlor. The Hat, as he said people called him for short, had gotten started on movies as we finished our slices, and movies for him meant vehicles for showcasing Steve McQueen. He listened to me talk a little about the movies I had watched with my old girlfriend at the Pioneer Theater, right around the corner, then said, that's great, that's great, but what about *Bullitt?* What about *The Great Escape?*

I told him I hadn't seen much Steve McQueen, but that I'd no doubt get around to it soon.

Soon? How about now? That was always my philosophy: fuck "soon," let's do it now. I got a player at home. You help me with the boxes and then we can watch some of the maestro. I got some Bud in the fridge. I live nearby.

Despite my protests, offered up more out of fatigue than anything, that I really didn't have time, The Hat made a beeline for the Steve McQueen section and selected a couple of fistfuls worth of tapes so that we could have "a choice for our viewing pleasure." He talked Steve McQueen exploits most of the way to his place, which was, indeed, nearby. He lived on Second Street, across from the Marble Cemetery.

Lupe, he said. It's me, open the door.

Lupe didn't come to the door this time, so he handed me the tapes and dug around in the pockets of his baggy old-guy pants until, about three minutes later, he came up with a key.

Now listen, he said. My sister's batteries upstairs are running down but she's all right. She's a good person. You allergic to cats?

I shook my head.

O.K., let's go in.

I know what I was expecting—some kind of East Village Lupe-haunted spider hole filled with the malodorous accumulation of decades stacked in every available space and threatening to breach the proverbial rafters—but that's not what I walked into. What I walked into was so clean and brightly lit and uncluttered that the shift my mind was forced to make from the clogged-toilet imagery it had been preparing itself for was unsettling.

It's nice, huh?

The Hat's fedora shone in a dazzling blend of natural and electric light and his eyes twinkled. The cats I'd seen before came sauntering out from under a row of chairs, flicked their tails a couple of times, and brushed themselves against our legs.

Lupe, The Hat said. We're going to get your fucking boxes. I got someone to help.

You want a beer?

I said I was fine but The Hat got me one anyway.

Lupe, he said again. We're going to get your boxes.

Lupe was in the closet. With the door closed. When The Hat pulled it open she walked out and past us without saying a word. When she got to the middle of the room she stopped and turned and stood looking in our direction. The cats came back from wherever they had swooshed off to and sat on either side of her. She had on the same filthy housedress she had been wearing before and I got hit with déjà vu so hard I felt like I needed to sit down. Instead I took a long swig of beer and wiped my forehead.

She likes that dress, she won't take it off, will you, Lupe?

Lupe didn't say anything.

She's got a whole fucking drawer full of dresses and she won't take that one off, The Hat said.

I wiped my forehead again.

The Hat asked me if I was all right, if I needed to take a break and maybe watch some Steve McQueen first before I got the boxes down. I told him it had been a late night and that I was under some job-related stress, but that I was perfectly fine.

Well, I know it would make Lupe happy if you could get them for her. She won't come out of the closet anymore.

I got the boxes down. There were three of them, good-sized, wedged hard onto the shelf above the coatrack. The Hat had me take them into the back bedroom, presumably Lupe's, which looked so spotless that but for the slightly warped floor and walls it could have belonged to a hotel. I set the boxes next to each other on the bed.

The Hat looked at them and shook his head. The tassel shook with it. It's just some of her old stuff. Stuff she picked up and had as a kid. She's been in that closet for a week. You want to sit down?

We went back into the living room. As soon as we had gotten there Lupe seemed to come alive. She beamed at her brother, then went to the bedroom and shut the door. The Hat sighed.

You got family?

No. Not anymore.

My kid sister. Used to be a beauty. Or anyway, not too bad. Once upon a time I had to crack some heads. Guys came sniffing. You wouldn't believe it to look at me now, but I used to be able to crack a head when I had to.

I told The Hat I needed to leave.

You don't want to watch *The Great Escape?* We can skip to the fence-jumping scene. It's got real tragedy, this one. I choke up every time.

I told him I was busy. I stifled a yawn, pressed my beer against the side of my face. My bed at The Fidelity was calling me. Fumes or no fumes. I told him maybe some other time.

Some other time is like *soon,* I know what that means. You don't get to be my age with a heart still beating without knowing some things. But, still, I'm grateful. Not everyone helps. I got a building full of yo-yos here. Won't even stop to answer you in the hallways. Next door I got nuts.

I thought of the nuts next door. Then I thought of the couple leaving Two Boots with the stroller, wondered what they were like, wondered if, through some fluke, or some serious upgrade in my customers, I'd be paying them a visit soon. The woman had been good-looking, exceptional, even, like some Greek movie star. The guy had been tall and beefy. Not bad-looking, but nothing like the woman. Cute kid too. I let myself flash for exactly one ridiculous second on me and Tulip pushing a stroller, maybe stopping for pizza, buying diapers for the baby, laughing, heading home, unloading groceries, giving the baby a bath. I then gave the scenario a quick run-through with the knockout, handsomely stomping her way down the avenues, in place of Tulip, then the contortionists, pushing the stroller with their feet, and almost laughed out loud.

Come here, Henry, I want to show you something, The Hat said.

He was standing next to what looked a little like a medicine cabinet sunk into the side wall. I raised my eyebrow, went over, and he opened it. There was a peephole there that looked out—at his insistence I bent over and put my eye to it—on the hallway. The Hat left my side, went around the corner, and reappeared in my line of sight. He took off his fedora and did a bow. Then he came back in.

You can't see it from the outside, he said. I got that from the old days. Some of us got them put in special. In the old days you didn't want to be inspecting your visitors through the balsa wood they got for doors in these places.

I guess not, I said.

Now it's just a convenience. Now if for example some guy, like you, Henry, comes and knocks at my neighbors', then stands and has some words with my sister, who has seen better days and can't answer right, I can see who it is.

Yeah? I said.

I don't mean I care, he said, not one way or the other, but with this thing and with my old habits I can keep my eyes open. Then I can think about the sounds I heard coming out of my neighbors' and put it together with things I've been hearing about jobs getting pulled in the neighborhood.

Jobs? I said.

You're pulling jobs, he said.

They're fake, it's a service, I said.

Sure, he said. But fake is funny, don't you think? Fake is like Steve McQueen and the movies—there's always a little real there too. Fake is never 100 percent. And sometimes fake is real.

He looked up at me for what felt like a long time, then he said, Kindt's working you good, huh?

I set my beer down on top of the peephole cabinet and told him it had been nice talking to him.

He's tough, huh, Aris Kindt? I never met him, not even in the old days, but I've been hearing things for years. Independent. Ran funny jobs. Always an angle, that one. Always smart. He'll fool you. He'll take care of you. He took care of a guy not too long ago. Guy who kept his books. Some accountant. That's what they say and that's what I heard. I heard you don't ever mess with him if you're smart.

We're friends, I said. It's not really business. He's retired. Someone else is running it. It's all fake.

Friends, said The Hat, and grinned. Like my good friends across the hall and in this building and in this neighborhood. I got so many friends I'm going to have a heart attack. What I also got is my sister, in there, looking through some boxes of junk, and a peephole in my wall so I can see who comes around and who is getting up to what exactly in this fucking city. I can look through this hole and see straight through the building. I can see you hitting yo-yos with salad bowls and getting yourself tattooed without knowing what was getting put on you and sleeping on the street and getting hit by trucks and running into blonds you got no idea about and meeting friendly Mr. Kindt. I can see that when you say you're busy, you mean you're going to go back to a flop and take a nap. I can see you pulling jobs and saying some quiet bullshit to my sister who can't answer you and I can see you looking at my hat now and saying, check out this old clown. Check out this old motherfucker who likes Steve McQueen. You want another beer? You want another beer, punk?

The Hat took a step toward me. I had the distinct feeling that he was going to produce a gun and put it in my face and pull the trigger and that there wouldn't be anything fake about it.

I've really got to go now, I said. I'm sorry for the trouble.

So go, Henry. I'm going to watch a movie. I'm going to watch Steve rock it on his bike. You should see the look on your face. You should go show it to your "friend." Go show it to Mr. Aris Kindt and see what he says. See what he says and leave this old clown with his hat and his sister in fucking peace.

TWENTY-SIX

A herring swims. A herring swims in a bucket. A herring swims in a blue bucket. A bright herring swims in a huge blue bucket. A herring moves forward. Why a herring and not some other fish? Because it's exquisite. Because the adult common herring, more properly known as *Clupea harengus,* is found in temperate cold waters of the North Atlantic and is about one foot or thirty centimeters long with silvery sides and a blue back.

Blue.

Yes, can you picture it? The female of the species lays up to fifty thousand tiny eggs, which sink to the sea bottom and develop there, the young maturing in about three years.

And then?

And then they rise.

Elevate.

Propagate forward and vertically through the deep and the dark by the millions.

So many.

Yes. And other fish come to feed upon them.

Eat them all?

Not all.

Most?

Yes, most, and in dying, it's quite lovely, they luminesce.

I'm not sure what you mean.

I mean they give off light as they die. As they drift off through the dark waters.

Do the immature fish luminesce?

I'm not sure. Probably.

And they're blue?

With silvery sides.

Most of them, as you say, are killed by other fish.

By other fish, yes, Henry, which is an utterly acceptable form . . .

Form of what?

Of undoing. Of annihilation.

Having said this, Mr. Kindt leaned far back into his chair, lifted his cigar, and took a long, ruminative puff.

Think of the beauty of it, Henry, he said. It happens over and over, and will continue to happen long after we are gone, long after we have laid aside our skin and bones or whatever it is we have here and have shuffled off.

Or stepped forward.

Out of our skin and into our shadow.

What about the fishing industry?

Of course, the fishing industry. Yes, that's true, the fishing industry complicates things, and has most certainly taken a hideous toll.

A hideous toll that puts that pickled herring into your mouth every day.

Mr. Kindt smiled. Oh, I'm simply full of contradictions, Henry, he said. Aren't you?

I shrugged. I wasn't sure what I was full of. A neat scalpel trench, some metal sutures, and a lot less morphine than usual, for starters. Besides Mr. Kindt, who had given me a little hit of Dilaudid so that I wouldn't, he said, go completely to pieces, I had seen no one apart from Aunt Lulu since my assignation with Dr. Tulp. Since the surgery, the slight correction, the scraping-out of some renegade flecks of lead, the "lightly invasive procedure, Henry" she had performed. After they had held me down and ripped my suit off me. After they strapped me to a gurney and rolled me down the hall.

Thanks for asking, I feel wonderful, I said.

I'm so very glad to hear it, Henry, Mr. Kindt said.

How was your tour of the ward with my aunt?

I'm sure she'll tell you all about it when she comes to see you, Henry.

I can't wait.

Oh, I suspect you can.

Mr. Kindt smiled.

I shuddered.

Cold? Mr. Kindt said. Funny, I am too. Or not funny. No, I don't think so. You see, not long after Lulu left, I had a visitor of my own. Someone I hadn't seen in many years. Most curious. He came and sat at the foot of my bed, much the way I often sit at the foot of yours. He was dressed in a pair of bathing trunks and dripped much more than seemed reasonable onto my sheets.

Who was it?

A young man. He reminded me much of myself in my own distant youth, except of course for the bathing trunks. And in fact he told me we shared a name.

So there is more than one of you here now.

Yes, but I don't get the feeling he will be visiting you.

Well that's a relief.

Yes, I suppose it must be. I wonder if he will drop in again? I suspect I should set out a towel.

Did you unload the merchandise?

I wouldn't be sitting here smiling so much and discussing the beauty and sadness of aquatic wonders if I hadn't. Or perhaps I should say I probably wouldn't. After all, it is my favorite subject.

Along with history.

Yes, along with history. The accumulation of remembered circumstance.

You mean the pile.

Do I?

Yes, the pile of dead fish. I don't feel very well, Mr. Kindt.

I know you don't, Henry.

Very early that morning, I had put on the robe with the fake ID card, limped through the halls of the ward, which, incidentally, had gone dim, not to say dark, again, and picked up the speed.

Mr. Kindt had come into my room four times before I had relented. Each time he had gotten angrier, less eloquent, more insistent. Each time he had brought up Aunt Lulu.

She's not at all like you described her to me, he said.

No comment, I said.

You need a little less juice in your system, Henry, it's clouding your judgment, he said.

So no one came around with my meds. Not even after I had pressed the button that was supposed to bring them, not after I had called out, not after I had walked down the hallways of the ward and out into the little garden and yelled. Deserted. All the terminal, critical, serious, and mild cases were gone, the machines in their rooms strangely mute, no longer pumping and blinking. Even Mr. Kindt's room was empty. I found a couple of loose cigars and a box of crackers. I lit one of the cigars and pressed the glowing end against the cracker box and burned a hole. Then I took a few crackers out and ate them. Or tried to eat them. It didn't work—I couldn't swallow, not even close. I spit what I had chewed into Mr. Kindt's toilet, flushed, and, still holding the cigar, walked out.

I went to Dr. Tulp's office and banged on the door for a while. Then sat on the floor, slumping considerably, my wound hurting hideously, expecting Aunt Lulu or who knows what to show up at any minute, and smoked.

Then I put on the robe and went to get the speed.

So maybe now . . . I said.

Oh, not quite yet, Henry, Mr. Kindt said. You made things quite difficult for me, you see. You made my position less certain, and even if it was only briefly, dear Henry, you will have to continue to pay for a time.

For how long?

Mr. Kindt shrugged. For a time. But you must think of it as an exchange—a simple transaction. Difficulty for difficulty. I would call it quite fair.

Like wampum and some hatchet heads for an island.

It's much less problematic a transaction than that one was, Mr. Kindt said.

I'll leave, I said. I'll get the fuck out of here.

Leave? Mr. Kindt said. Leave here? None of us get to leave. Don't be outrageous. That's just silly, Henry.

It was. I didn't completely know that yet, but that is certainly how it has turned out.

O.K., fine, I'll talk to Dr. Tulp.

Do so. Yes, *please* do.

Dr. Tulp, who was back in her office, barely looked up at me over her papers.

I'm very busy, Henry, she said.

Like last night.

Yes, she said, like last night, like today, like tomorrow. This is a hospital in a city where hospitals are much needed, perhaps now more than ever. A hospital is a center of learning and healing. Here we are in the business of casting light into the shadows, of banishing trauma, of soothing hurts. How is the incision?

It's great. I'm just fantastic. I really appreciate your concern.

It was necessary, Henry. It will help. You were drifting. I suspect it will lead you back on track.

Dr. Tulp's eyes, which had flipped up for a moment, went back to her papers. I stood up. Dr. Tulp's hand moved toward the buzzer that would bring the attendants. I sat back down.

My aunt, I said.

Dr. Tulp raised an eyebrow.

Never mind. Forget that. I don't want to talk about her. Mr. Kindt.

Dr. Tulp straightened her papers and put them down.

My friend. He's changed. I offended him. He's getting out of control. He says he's got his own visitor now. A guy in swim trunks. Is there a pool here? I think it's supposed to mean something.

Sorry, Henry, I don't follow you.

It's me. I'm the one who's been ripping this place off. Mr. Kindt took over for Job. I pissed him off.

Slow down, Henry.

He's withholding my meds.

No one is withholding your medication, Henry.

Yes, someone definitely the fuck is.

No, Henry, Dr. Tulp said.

See, my boy, said Mr. Kindt when I returned. There is unfortunately absolutely nothing your beautiful young Dr. Tulp will do.

No, I don't think there is.

I looked at him.

Well, I said.

Yes, dear boy? he asked.

I shut my eyes. I counted to fifty then opened them. He was still there. I took a deep breath. I sighed.

You could at least apologize for calling me a little shit earlier, I said.

Did I call you a little shit? After all it doesn't quite sound like me, does it? Not quite the variety of vocabulary I would elect to employ.

I shook my head. It didn't. It sounded like Aunt Lulu. Mr. Kindt took a step toward me and took my hands in his.

I am not the one who needs to apologize to you for any-thing, Henry, am I? he said. Not for anything, relatively speaking, too serious?

No, I suppose not, I said.

I think my apologies, if there are to be any, will be directed elsewhere—toward my poor wet young man. In fact perhaps I should slip off for a time and see if I can't make myself more available to him.

Mr. Kindt gave a nervous little laugh, like a lightbulb breaking, like a tiny frozen fist shattering against a wall.

I nodded and squeezed his soft, near-translucent hands.

Ah, my dear Henry, my dear, dear Henry, I sense we are starting to understand each other, he said.

TWENTY-SEVEN

The night of Mr. Kindt's murder it rained hard. I had a couple of drinks at the Horseshoe and watched the rain beat down on the park and finally wondered, with more than a mild sense of unease, what I'd gotten myself into. It's not that I wasn't happy enough to help Mr. Kindt out with his little fantasy, but after the events of the past week, since the night with Tulip, since my visit to Mel the Hat's and his various insights, since a meeting with Cornelius and the others on, as Cornelius put it, the various modalities of the crime, not to mention my encounter with the proposed victim himself and the subsequent revelations about the famous night on Lake Otsego, my brain was really chewing at things, and these things did not taste good.

Sitting there, it seemed to me I could trace the beginning of the decidedly unpleasant taste to the latter portion of my night with Tulip, which is when, though I didn't give it much thought until after my encounter with The Hat, I finally learned something concrete about the circumstances of her relationship with Mr. Kindt.

After our chat at Grand Central, Tulip and I had made our way back to the tattoo parlor on Orchard, where we poured ourselves shots from a bottle of Ketel One and toasted Cornelius, the knockout, the knockout's formidable cleavage, the flexibility of the contortionists, my new tattoo, and, most of all, Mr. Kindt. On the subject of this latter, Tulip took pains to stress that she really had been stretching things into the realm of the speculative when she had offered me Mr. Kindt's presumptive biography and, in high spirits, I lied and told her that Mr. Kindt's origins didn't matter to me in the least. He had been an extraordinarily generous friend, almost a patron, and if the 1 + 1 of some night on some lake didn't feel like adding up to 2 then that was fine with me. Tulip said it was also fine with her—that if he had been a patron to me, he had been that and more to her in the time that she had known him. Which, I asked her, had been how long? She raised an eyebrow, started some kind of count on her fingers, stopped, shrugged, and said that it hadn't been that long.

How long is that? I said.

Cornelius introduced me a month or so before I met you, she said. How long ago was that?

Cornelius introduced you to Mr. Kindt? I said.

She shrugged and took a sip of her drink. Then she toasted Anthony, the inept but very handsome first murderer. We drained our glasses, then Tulip put the bottle away, grabbed my hand, sunk a fingernail into it, and grabbed the back of my head.

It had been a *very* long time since anything like Tulip on that night in that back room had happened to me and by the time we were done and she had put on her t-shirt and gone to get herself another shot, I was lying in a heap extruding sweat, etc., and panting and feeling pretty magnificent. As I said previously, it was only the next day, as I was walking around the neighborhood in a daze, like someone had borrowed my brain and stuck an old cream-filled donut in its place, that any kind of even low-grade analytical thinking process kicked in. But after I left The Hat's, and had poured a few midafternoon beverages on the paranoid feelings my visit and his peephole and commentary had produced, I went home and back to wallowing around in what, by the time I fell asleep in/was knocked out by the hot dog cart fumes, I had only half-convinced myself were probably just the symptoms of uncertainty inherent in any budding romance, let alone one taking root in the context of mock murders and so forth.

Anyway, my limping mind had gone on melting in and out of a sense of unease around the Tulip question. And sitting there at the Horseshoe that night, I kept coming back to the fact that she had only known Mr. Kindt for a little longer than I had, and that Cornelius had introduced her to him.

I hadn't gotten much more to go on about this at my meeting with Cornelius and Co., though there had been plenty of information of a more general nature, especially in retrospect, to make my eyebrows tick up a notch or two.

This meeting had taken place the day before the murder at one of the outside tables at Veselka, and had started with Cornelius stressing to me that Mr. Kindt didn't want to see me until after the job had been completed, that this was an important part of the scenario and should be adhered to.

Why? I said.

That's the script, Cornelius said.

But I always see him.

Not before the murder.

The knockout and the contortionists were present at this get-together, which, like my conversation with the knockout at the Odessa, possessed a certain hard-boiled feeling that I will do my best to evoke, though not, in this case, I should stress, at the *conscious* expense of substantive or incidental accuracy: we are too deep into these sad, blurry proceedings for that. The knockout had on a black raincoat and a black miniskirt and kept crossing and uncrossing her legs, saying goddamn it, and sucking, almost slurping, on cigarettes, so that Cornelius finally told her to either take it easy or leave. For their part, the contortionists, dressed in matching purple velour tracksuits, had arrived late, then immediately settled into unpleasant leg and body positions and wouldn't stop staring at me.

You're all making me nervous, I finally said.

He's nervous, one of the contortionists said.

I had a run-in yesterday, I said. With a guy called Mel the Hat. Old-timer. Anyone ever hear of him?

Mel the Hat? Is that a joke? the knockout said.

No, I've never heard of him. Now remember to hit him hard, said Cornelius, who had already run through the scenario once and was going over it a second time.

I heard you the first time, I said.

Once you've got the tape around him you smack him on the side of the head with the big ashtray and then you pull the wire tight around his throat.

Are you ladies going to be there? I asked the contortionists.

Us ladies, they said. Flicking their eyebrows up.

Just you, said Cornelius. You won't need any help with him.

This proved true. When I pulled him out of bed the night of the murder, he smiled, and said, my dear boy, and let me push him into the front room.

What about for moral support?

At this, the knockout picked up her cigarette and jammed it into her mouth, then two-fingered a shard of lettuce and flicked some of the dill dressing coating it onto the ground.

If you don't mind my pointing it out, you guys seem a little agitated, I said to Cornelius after we had all watched the knockout slip the lettuce shard past the cigarette into her mouth.

Unrelated, Cornelius said.

Nothing to fucking do with you, said the knockout.

That's right, Mr. Nervous, said the contortionists.

Fine, I said.

I asked if I could have a copy of the scenario.

Cornelius said I could not.

That's why I've been going over it with you, Henry, he said. Oral instructions only, no record—safe. Just like every other time we've done this.

I had written instructions the first couple of times.

Yeah, big deal, what did they say?

Why isn't Tulip here?

Why would she be here? said the knockout. Why does he think Tulip should be here, Cornelius?

Cornelius said he didn't know why I thought Tulip should be there.

I said maybe because she (1) apparently had known him for quite some time and was probably either working for or with him and (2) was a key player in the scenario.

He can count, said the knockout.

I've known her for a while, said Cornelius. She's a friend. Then he said Tulip wasn't there because she already knew what she was supposed to do. Her presence had not been required because her role in the affair was merely ancillary and did not involve the scene of the crime.

She practically lives with him, I said.

Not according to the scenario. According to the scenario she lives on Orchard Street, behind the tattoo parlor.

Yeah, I know about that place, I said. I know about the back room. We're getting pretty friendly, me and Tulip.

No one said anything.

Very friendly, I said.

Jesus Christ, make this guy stop with the commentary, said the knockout.

That's your business, Henry, Cornelius said. We don't care about that. Just stick to the scenario.

She gave me a tattoo, I said.

Tell him to shut up, Cornelius, the knockout said.

I just thought you guys would be interested, that's all. Aren't you guys interested? I said to the contortionists.

They didn't answer.

Yeah, yeah, we're all real interested, the knockout said. Henry finally got a piece of ass.

O.K., said Cornelius, placing a hand on the table, does anyone have anything germane to say? Otherwise this meeting is adjourned.

I looked at the knockout. She looked at her fingernails, which were tapping away on the table in front of her.

Why? I said.

What do you mean, why? said Cornelius.

I mean why am *I* murdering Mr. Kindt?

You already asked Tulip that.

Yeah, she told me a ton. Real helpful. I'm going to write

a book. Incidentally, she referred, in this illuminating chronicle, to the fact that Mr. Kindt comes from Cooperstown.

So what, he does. We've already talked about this.

So what I'm asking you is, does this murder I'm supposed to carry out have anything to do with Cooperstown?

What are you, Sherlock Holmes? You're getting paid. Mind your fucking business.

How do you say that in French?

Plus you're a real joker.

O.K., never mind, let me ask you this—does it matter if I know or don't know about what happened in Cooperstown or what, exactly, you and Mr. Kindt are up to?

Cornelius paused here. He looked at the knockout. She looked at the contortionists. They shrugged.

No, it doesn't matter, Henry.

But you aren't going to tell me?

Cornelius shrugged.

All right, forget it, how about the first question?

The first question?

Why?

Because he wants you to.

He wants *me* to?

Yeah, *he* fucking wants you to, you fucking sad ass.

This last remark surprised me. Because it wasn't said by the knockout, it was said by one of the contortionists.

Whoa, I said.

This is getting very, very fucking boring, the other contortionist said.

O.K., I won't bore you much longer. But I do want to know if this whole thing, this whole thing about me committing murders, was a lead-up to this? To killing Mr. Kindt tomorrow night?

I don't know, said Cornelius, lying. You'll have to ask him.

Obviously, when Cornelius told me I would have to ask Mr. Kindt, he meant after the murder, when it wouldn't matter anymore. But as it turned out, I got to ask him before. That very afternoon, in fact. My brain, having found a rare felicitous moment, was starting to whir away about Tulip and murder and the mattress in the back room and the look on the contortionists' faces and the supposed importance of this particular job, and the still-unexplained murk about the old business on Lake Otsego, and as I was sitting over a burger at Stingy Lulu's on St. Mark's Place, I got the urge to go over and see my friend.

In connection with this impromptu visit, and the little detail that Mr. Kindt was in a bad way during it, I'll relate that one night over several brandies and a couple of cigars, Mr. Kindt, in vintage Mr. Kindt fashion, told me it had been said that the body, in dying, releases a thick white mist, which until that point has been held by mysterious forces within the skin. He did not say what this mist was for or why dying released it, but did note that it tended to gather in the mind when its host was sleeping, and that, in some instances, especially in the case of those "not long for this terrible earth," did not leave the mind even after the host was awake. He then said he had more than once, when wide-awake, experienced a curious phenomenon that could be attributed to such a mist. When it happened, people and objects tended to lose their definition and bleed into each other, an erosion of border and contour he found very troubling. On those days, he canceled all his appointments and stayed inside, eyes closed, barely moving, as contexts and circumstances that had long seemed inviolable to him came unhinged. It was, he told me, partly to preempt the noxious effects of these occasional bouts that he had taken to admitting a greater-than-average measure of calculated falsification into his life.

That was all I had gotten out of him on the subject that day, but when I went to visit him when I wasn't supposed to I got a little more. It was a bright afternoon in Manhattan, and the cool air as I went through the park smelled like it is supposed to, or you think it is supposed to, on a cool bright day in a small city park; by that I mean something like *almost* fresh, so that, in a way that was totally unrelated to what I was thinking about, I felt pretty good. For a few minutes, my mind ceased its whirring and my unease took a break and I was just some guy with a pretty good job walking across the park on a sunny day. I thought about this afterward, after leaving Mr. Kindt's, about having felt, for those few minutes crossing the park and walking into his building, almost, as I say, good, or, as I put it, *pretty* good, and I thought about it while I sat in the bar looking out at the rain over the same park, at the glowing lamps and dark trunks and wet benches, getting ready to murder him. It wasn't like I left Mr. Kindt's that afternoon feeling awful—I didn't. It's just that after I had left him, especially the first time, I definitely no longer felt "pretty good," and walking through the park wasn't going to help.

Anyway, still sucking in reasonably fresh air, I left the park, crossed Avenue B, and let myself into his building. I took the stairs two at a time, started to knock, and discovered the door was open. I went in. It didn't take long to realize that Mr. Kindt's mist or whatever was gnawing away at him, because when I said, hey, buddy (he was sitting, hatless, heart monitor in his lap, in a black rocker by the window), how about some herring? he started to scream.

Mr. Kindt, hey, I said.

I could barely hear myself say this. His hands were gripping the arms of the rocker like he wanted to splinter them.

Hey, I said, starting to move toward him.

His eyes widened and he began rocking violently back and forth and stomping his legs on the floor.

All right, I said, moving away. I'll come back later.

I left. I walked around the park. I did not feel good. Not awful, but not good.

About an hour later I went back. Before I had a chance to say anything, Mr. Kindt smiled, and said, I know, my dear boy, I'm sorry, and I may start screaming again at any moment, but what came in the door speaking about herring wasn't you, although for the first time in a very long while I was me.

I looked at him.

I suppose that's not going to be very easy to understand, is it? he said.

He definitely seemed calmer. He had put his hat on and left the rocker, which was lying on its side in a tangle with the heart monitor.

You were screaming pretty loud there, I said.

I know, Henry, it came over me, and as I say it may well come over me again. Incidentally, you know, I very much like it when you call me buddy. Even in the state I was in I found that very calming.

Well sure, buddy, I'm glad you do.

Yes, I like it very much, he said.

I'll call you that whenever you like. I'll spread the word.

Call me buddy now.

O.K., buddy, I said.

I called him buddy a couple more times, then he said that that was enough for the time being and I agreed and changed the subject.

What did you mean a minute ago when you said "I was me?"

Well, it might be too hard to explain that just at the moment, Henry.

Can you try?

No, I don't think I can. I think it might precipitate another, you know, my boy, screaming episode.

From the mist?

Yes, he said. I suppose it is.

While we were talking, he had opened a plastic container, one of several spread across the coffee table, and had begun putting generous amounts of creamed herring and onion onto crackers.

The herring you mentioned, he said. It was a lovely idea.

I'm glad, I said, taking a cracker and putting it in my mouth. Delicious. A little warm maybe, but good.

Listen, I said, I'd like to ask you something.

Mr. Kindt put a cracker in his mouth and looked at me.

Well, Henry, as I say, I may not be able to answer or talk about certain questions.

O.K., how about I ask the question and you decide whether or not you want to answer?

That sounds reasonable.

All right, buddy, what I'm wondering, and what I asked Cornelius and he wouldn't answer . . .

Mr. Kindt raised a finger. Perhaps no more buddy now in this context, he said.

Fine, no problem, I said. Anyway, what I asked Cornelius was whether or not this whole murder gig thing I've been doing was just a lead-up to this—to, you know, bumping you off. If, you know, the whole thing was to prepare me, to lend authenticity, as you put it, to the big job, which was you.

Mr. Kindt put another cracker in his mouth.

Why do you want to know this, Henry? he said after he had swallowed.

I'm feeling kind of uncomfortable with the whole thing, I said.

I'm sorry to hear that.

I had kind of an ultimately pretty sour meeting with a guy called Mel the Hat.

Now there is a name.

He said you were tough. And tricky.

Oh well, I suppose I am. Or was.

He said he knew about you from the old days. Said you had a reputation. That you took care of people, had even taken care of someone recently. I was wondering if, maybe, you know, you were planning on taking care of or tricking me in some way.

Mr. Kindt picked up the last cracker and handed it to me.

That's for you, buddy, he said, smiling.

I took it, told myself that that was his way of answering, smiled back, and pushed the conversation off in another direction.

Tulip and I got together, I said. Two nights ago.

Oh, did you really? he said.

Yes.

And? Was it lovely?

It was.

Excellent.

Yes, excellent. Absolutely. But . . .

Yes?

What I'm wondering is, what I can't stop asking myself is, why did Tulip sleep with me?

I would have thought she or Cornelius would have told you. It's part of your motivation. She has now, to paraphrase the script, seduced you and told you that there is a portfolio of valuable documents under the floorboard along that wall.

Cornelius told me.

Good. The board is loose. When you leave, after the job has been completed, take the portfolio with you. Then go and see Tulip.

Right, I said. But, I mean, she really did sleep with me. Not fake. Not, you know, mock. Not part of the scenario. We, ahem, tussled.

Oh well, said Mr. Kindt, I have always entertained hopes that the two of you would become better acquainted. If the fulfillment of my little scenario has helped move you in that direction, that is wonderful, that is really just fine. All my blessings, as it were.

Really?

Mr. Kindt said, yes, my boy, really, then suggested that it was time for me to take my leave.

I'll be going then, I said.

Yes, until tomorrow night, he said.

So, I'm going to murder you.

I'm counting the seconds.

It's not going to be pretty.

I certainly hope not.

Beautiful maybe, but not pretty.

That sounds perfect, Henry.

I'm going to hit you hard.

Oh yes, good. Don't hold back. It must both look and *feel* authentic. The feeling is what is essential. The feeling is what I am after. I woke up last week and thought, I just have to be killed. That will do it. It won't *undo* it, of course. But it will help.

Help what?

Never mind, Henry. I'm just thinking aloud.

Do you want to run through it now?

No, I don't think that will be necessary. You know where everything is? The ashtray? The bag of my blood to splatter around?

I nodded. He smiled. We stood there looking at each other.

As I walked down the stairs, out the door, and over to the park, I thought of him, screaming and rocking and stuffing crackers in his mouth and calling me dear boy and limping slightly and paying my way into museums. As these images played before me, and as I registered how very differently I felt now than I had after leaving Stingy Lulu's and walking across the park earlier, my mind turned simultaneously to the aforementioned films my old girlfriend and I had once taken in at the Pioneer, next to Two Boots. They had consisted almost entirely of light playing off water, and water playing off people, as they themselves played at running through bars of light. Children had run past the camera and thrown shadows onto attic walls, or swung sticks back and forth through blue-tinted air, and we had left the theater with the sensation that projector light was gushing out of our eyes. For a moment, this remembered light poured onto Mr. Kindt, the one my mind held out before me, making him almost completely translucent, a kind of ghost of photons and dust motes and bands of fine shadow. It was just as this image was about to dissolve into glittering nothingness that Mr. Kindt himself, ever full of surprises, came up beside me, said, hello again, buddy, wiped a little oil from the corner of his mouth, and took my arm.

TWENTY-EIGHT

Nothing ever happens the way you say it does—we can agree on that, right? I mean something happens to you and then you tell it and you've just told something different from the something that happened and that's what people hear and they say, oh, that "monstrous, miscomprehending, appearance-believing" creep. Or that's what you hear. You tell it to yourself. You go to the store and you buy a pound of flour and some crackers and then you say to yourself, even if only casually, I went to the store and I bought a pound of flour and some cookies, I'm hungry, maybe I'll have one, despite the fact that I'm a "monstrous, miscomprehending, appearance-believing" creep. So a cracker is not a cookie, even if for some people it might be an adequate substitute. However, I am not one of those people and I don't particularly like crackers, I have no idea why I would buy them. And the flour, that's also a mystery. Why a pound of flour? To make cookies? My favorites are peanut butter and peanut butter chocolate chip. My god I used to love the way Carine would put on her French accent and say *chocolate:* "cho co let." But I don't have any peanut butter. Not here. And I don't like crackers except with herring. So I went out to buy herring and instead I bought flour. I succeeded in getting the crackers, even in getting a good brand of crackers, Carr's, I believe, so there you have it.

Have what, Henry?

I'll give you a better example. Take the vanishing of Mr. Kindt. When I said that the last time I saw him he had let go of my hands and vanished, I meant something very different. I meant something more like diminishing.

So Mr. Kindt did not vanish?

No, Mr. Kindt diminished.

Explain.

I mean he was still there—not immediately, I grant you, he did do the thin-air thing then went away for a few days, or whatever you would call them, to make himself available to his swimmer, but soon enough he was back. He was back, but his eyes were no longer such a pretty blue and his neck seemed to have straightened and he didn't talk to me anymore about stealing and withholding meds. Even when I brought these subjects up, he acted like he hadn't heard me.

In what way was he there?

He's still there. You want to go see him? Maybe we can catch him conversing with his wet friend.

Later. In what way is he there?

He comes to my room, like before, only he doesn't get in my bed and watch TV with me anymore, and he doesn't show any interest in cigars or Hank Williams or in eating herring.

What does he do?

He talks. He stands by the window and looks out through the black netting and talks about the same old things. The things he used to talk about. Before.

Like what?

Like himself. Like mist. Drifting out over everything. Blurring all the borders. Or like annihilation. About having annihilated someone and through that annihilation having been himself annihilated in the exact center point of his meaning, like herring that are annihilated as they are rising.

But he is no longer interested in eating the fish?

That's what I said.

But you are?

I've picked up the habit. It's almost like an addiction.

What is Mr. Kindt doing here, Henry?

It wasn't me.

Then you persist.

Of course I persist.

Inadvisable, but that's not what we're discussing here.

What are we discussing here?

Your ongoing relationship with Mr. Kindt. Since his murder. His great interest in you.

Well what about the wet guy's interest in him?

Again, that is not the conversation we are having.

You're right. I'm sorry. Still, I don't know why he's bothering me. If anything, I ought to be bothering him.

Why do you say that?

I don't quite know, it's just a sense that whatever happened was part of an exchange. But I can't quite get there. Just like Mr. Kindt can't quite figure out the swimmer yet. I was thinking maybe I would ask my aunt, if she ever comes back. Maybe she could help. Maybe she's figured out how it all works.

I'm not sure she has, Henry.

I'm not sure either, but anyway, as you said, we were discussing Aris Kindt. My Aris Kindt. In all his diminished splendor. Would you like to hear more about him? Would that help further our discussion, push us forward, get us somewhere? Shall I play the part, try on the mask, do my dear dead friend, do Aris, as over and over again Aris does himself?

All right.

I was born in seventeenth-century Leiden, where I grew up in solitude, left, by my family, to my own devices, except for the many beatings my father administered. We drank milk in great quantities when it was to be had, and I can still hear the sound of butter being made and smell the churn. My father was a quiver maker, which I became after him although I was not so deeply blessed in this capacity with skill. My mother was a darling woman. My father beat her once too often and she left a scarlet trail across the snow. Then I left Leiden forever because I had to. It was not a lovely life and I used to poach ducks from the canals and for a time lived in an abandoned windmill. That isn't true. For a time I lived in the most miserable of hovels. My dream was to go to Amsterdam. It was difficult to go to Amsterdam. I kept getting caught. Once I beat a man. Too much. Once also there was an incident involving a young woman. Many incidents. I disliked death. Too much mist. Some nights I would dream about my father and young sister. Also I would dream of New Amsterdam. It was truly new then and every boy had seen the great triple-masters in their dreams. Once I stole a potion from a very old man in Maastricht. I drank the potion and fell into a dream. In the dream I saw a man much like myself lying in a ditch at the edge of a green field covered with frost. I went up to the man and kicked him and he awoke. It was me.

Who do you mean by "me"?

Mr. Kindt. The centuries-old version.

All right, continue.

It's you, the sleeping man said. I was just dreaming about you. In my dream you were lying in a field just like this one. Oh, I said. Actually, there was never any potion. There was a theft, but it was brandy I stole. I woke up in the field. Cold. I was freezing. I returned to town and tried to steal a man's cape. The man was a magistrate. I seemed to be in Amsterdam. Then I was hung. A thick mist swirled around me. Then I was harrowed. In a great hall with high dark ceilings and candles and glass jars and an audience in attendance. I was on a stage, on a slab, and a painter had been commissioned to paint me, to paint them.

Rembrandt.

Yes, Rembrandt. The painting is called *The Anatomy Lesson*. My German author gives much thought to the matter, conjectures that Rembrandt secretly sympathized with Mr. Kindt, saw the violence that had been done to him.

To you.

No. Not to me. Well, yes, to me with this mask on. It's a little convoluted. Let me take it off for a second. Consider it taken off. O.K., there was a historical Mr. Kindt. A petty thief named Aris Kindt who was hung then dissected then painted by Rembrandt.

With whom you identify.

I'm just Henry again.

With whom Mr. Kindt identified. They shared a name.

Yes. Mr. Kindt, my Mr. Kindt, had borrowed the name from a certain Mr. Kindt who had only used it for some weeks.

Borrowed it?

Let's just say that the temporary user of the name didn't need it anymore.

How many Mr. Kindts are there?

At least three, only one of whom, to the best of our knowledge, could swim, but now it's only the first one that matters.

Why?

Ask Mr. Kindt.

He's dead, Henry.

Who isn't?

Dr. Tulp made a note in her book then looked at me.

Anything else?

Lots. Descartes was there, they say, as was, possibly, Sir Thomas Browne. Did you know that in those days we still believed that after death one could feel pain? I certainly could. Most excruciating were the extremities. The first thing he did was to open up my arm.

Or at least, Dr. Tulp said, in the painting the first thing that has been opened is the arm.

Yes, in the painting. Of course a real dissection, as my German writer points out, would begin with the intestines—those areas most given to decomposition. Regardless, there was vigorous applause. I understood the larger part of the audience had been expecting a lesson in female rather than male anatomy—it is female rather than male anatomy that excites in this context, but then what is the gender of the dead? During the lesson, I learned the verb *extirpate*. Do you know it?

Yes, Henry, I know it.

What I had tried to do was steal the man's cape.

I think it is time to stop now with this, Henry—you said yourself the mask is off. We've done enough for now.

Dr. Tulp was there.

I am Dr. Tulp, Henry.

Dr. Nicolas Tulp of the Royal Dutch Academy, who regularly performed such dissections for the benefit of Amsterdam's intelligentsia, so that light would replace shadow and their minds would be freed of mist. Little matter that in the center of this, so to speak, sweeping-away of the cobwebs lay a small, recently breathing body.

We have no indication, outside of Rembrandt's painting, that Aris Kindt was a particularly small man.

I'm small.

No, Henry, you are not. You are quite average.

Well then never mind.

Where is Mr. Kindt right now, Henry?

Oh, he's around.

But diminished.

Somewhat. Dr. Tulp?

Yes, Henry.

Should I expect you to begin diminishing, so you can take care of your own business, or will you stick around for the odd chat and to perform the occasional minor or major surgery? I guess what I am wondering is, why, Dr. Tulp, are you here? *How* did you get here?

Dr. Tulp smiled, a little coldly, and didn't answer.

I looked around the brightly lit office, with its rows and rows of folders and dull, worn office furniture, and shuddered.

I'd like to go home, I said. To Carine and the cats.

This is where you live now, Henry.

Can it, fairly, be called living?

What would you like to call it?

Have you scheduled any more surgeries? Any more scouring and filing and cleaning?

A few. There is more scraping to be done. We must be sure that all the lead is gone.

Am I still going to be moving on?

Eventually, Henry, but not just yet. I feel you've made a breakthrough, and it must be encouraged. I have filed for a postponement.

A reprieve.

If you like.

Until they hook me up to a machine and put me behind bars, boil my head, tear me asunder, chop off my hands.

What you did was very serious, Henry. Murder is serious, there are consequences. These are the consequences.

What did you do, Dr. Tulp? Are these your consequences too? Do you have any visitors? Am *I* your visitor? Is that it? Am I going to get to perform some surgery on you?

She smiled.

You are making progress, Henry, she said. And, unfortunately for me, I suspect, it will all become more and more clear as you continue to reflect on it. Perhaps you should set the results of your reflections down on paper. I will make sure you get some. I have thought of doing the same thing myself. There is so much I'm unsure of. You will see. I think we all will. There is light pouring into the darkness, flooding the corridors. It is moving more quickly now.

TWENTY-NINE

We walked then, arm in arm around the East Village, and as we wove our way past bus stops and beat-up garbage cans and derelict water fountains and the constantly, abruptly changing vectors of people moving forward, Mr. Kindt leaned in close to me and talked. He started by explaining that "by chance" Cornelius had phoned him just after I had left and that they had conferred and agreed that I might as well know the story of their night together "all those years ago," that knowing it might help set my mind at ease, might allay my fears of being tricked "and so forth," while at the same time producing the "happy result" of admitting me into an even greater measure of complicity with "my friends."

For we are your friends, Henry, Mr. Kindt said. Your dear friends, and none dearer, of course, than myself.

I said I felt the same way and wanted very much to know what had happened, but didn't want to precipitate another screaming episode. Mr. Kindt waved his free hand in a dismissive way, said he felt much better now, that a little stroll in the neighborhood would set him to rights and that I shouldn't worry about him at all.

All right, I said.

Good, he said.

Now I want you to picture, Henry, a town of fine homes and half-lit streets undulating on the banks of a shining lake and in this town two ambitious young men, who have met, shall we say, a third young man, and formed a happy triangle. This third point in the triangle is passing through town, making his circuitous way to New York from the Netherlands, with a valise containing an impressive number of valuable bonds. Can you picture it? Can you smell the late summer air, still warm, though shot through with the hint of autumn coming on? Can you admire the juxtaposition of three young men up to nothing terribly good in that lovely, quiet town next to those lovely, quiet waters? Now, never mind, dear boy, how we met this young man with his valise—let's just say that Cornelius had his ear to the proverbial ground and that both of us were already involved in certain aspects of the trade that made us, on the face of it, unthreatening to others in our line. Suffice it to say that we approached this young man and offered him a number of drinks, first in his hotel room and then in an establishment we knew and then down on the banks of Lake Otsego. We entered into a kind of confidence as we drank, and it was on those banks that this young man pulled a rumpled reproduction from his pocket, unfolded it, pointed to the corpse lying at its center, and told us it was his favorite painting. He loved it so much that he had borrowed the name of the painting's "hero," the corpse he was pointing to, for the purposes of the bit of business he was attending to. He spoke at some length, not quite but almost slurring his words, about how strangely thrilling it was to be using a new name, one that had belonged to the dead individual who lay at the center of Rembrandt's famous painting. He had had false documents made and was now, for the duration of his journey to New York City and perhaps, who knew, he said, beyond, called Aris Kindt.

Ah, I said.

And you see I looked very much like him and still had that touch of a Dutch accent.

Your namesake.

Mr. Kindt nodded. Yes, and carrying around a reproduction of a likeness of *his* namesake. He looked upon this tattered image of a man whose face is cast in shadow and who has been torn open in the name of progress with great fondness, almost tenderness. In speaking of this dead man, who had been so profoundly violated, he evoked Goethe's notion of elective affinities and marveled that of all the people in the wide world he might have felt drawn to it was this Aris Kindt, this dead, dissected man. It's a nice name, isn't it? he asked us. And I thought to myself, yes, it certainly is.

You killed him.

In a manner of speaking. He was a swimmer, you see. He got it into his head—well, we helped with this—that he wanted to show us just what a very fine swimmer he was. So we all went out onto the lake. Cornelius and I in a sort of canoe. He made it surprisingly far. In fact he very nearly reached the opposite shore. Then I became Aris Kindt.

And Cornelius?

I completed the delivery and we shared the proceeds. But I kept the name. And took full advantage of the surprisingly large network of contacts that came with the successful completion of the assignment. I made, as they say, good. Every now and again Cornelius has come to me and suggested that to ensure the healthy ongoing maintenance of our insoluble complicity we embark on a joint venture.

I have always agreed. History binds us all and dashes us together whether we know it or like it. Shared history adds the intricacy of love to the arrangement.

We had stopped at the corner of Third and Seventh. Cars and cabs swept past. I saw the woman with the green hair and piercings heading toward Cooper Union with her dog.

That's quite a story, I said.

It is, isn't it, Henry, Mr. Kindt said.

Hell of a story, I thought as I sat there the night of the murder, feeling uneasy, watching the rain fall.

Yes, I said.

And now you have entered more completely into our intricacy, Mr. Kindt said.

I'm more completely complicit, I said.

Murder me well, Henry, Mr. Kindt said.

Then, though it wasn't time yet, I got up and walked out the door.

Not sure what to do, I stuffed my hands in my pockets, crossed Seventh, and went into the park. After the thick, smoky air of the bar, the cold rain felt good, and I set off at a brisk pace. Tompkins Square Park—where I seem to have spent so much time over the course of these pages— is made up of a series of meandering asphalt paths that lead into open areas and wider lanes and surround fenced-off enclosures that contain a surprising number of trees and plants. Until not too many years ago, when they were forcibly evicted, the park was a haven for the homeless, but now on a rainy night you can pretty much walk the curved paths alone, seeing only the occasional cop or fellow stroller or worn-out drunks huddled together under beat-up umbrellas. It is a dreamy, slightly otherworldly place at night, and from time to time it plays host to vendors of odd comestibles, so I was not too surprised to round a bend and come upon a sweet-potato vendor set up beneath a lavender umbrella in the glow of one of the park lamps. As I passed, the woman behind the glistening, steaming metal cart called out "sweet potatoes, warm sweet potatoes" in a high, clear voice and almost before I knew what I was doing I had handed over a dollar and accepted one of the foil-wrapped potatoes, pulled it open, and taken a bite. The potato was incredibly sweet and moist and for a moment I stood under the heavy foliage of an oak tree, chewing, swallowing, and drifting—out over the city, the beautiful dirty rivers, the drenched islands, the roiled ocean.

But the cold rain and the calories I was consuming were waking me up, so it's not surprising, delicious, unlooked-for sweet potato or not, that my mind turned wearily, uneasily, back to love and intricacy and complicity, to silver bowls, dreams of Dutch polders, a look lifted directly from Rembrandt's painting, wacko stuff about life in the Netherlands in the seventeenth century, fake and real murders, gangsteresque behavior in restaurants, sextants, anatomy books, bottled plants, organs, Tulip, Cornelius, a death by drowning in the dark waters of Lake Otsego fifty years ago, and my dear friend, a confessed killer, lucid one moment, clearly mad as a fucking hatter, rocking back and forth at the center of his machine of mist and falsification, the next.

The rain hit the top of my head and the sugar from the potato smashed into my system and I thought about murders and Mr. Kindt taking care of someone, some accountant, and about Mel the Hat and his peephole, and about how, as he had said, nothing was ever 100 percent fake, there was always some real there. It was this principle, I thought, that gave some validity to Mr. Kindt's belief that somehow or other submitting himself to a particularly rigorous version of the murder procedure would help to alleviate a guilt spurred by the aftershocks of a violation that reached deep into the past. And there was something there, something in Mr. Kindt's wish to be mock murdered, maybe something just tangentially related that I hadn't grasped, something that involved me. Involved Cornelius and Co., including Tulip. Involved Mr. Kindt running out after me to relate, in overwhelming detail, a story he had declined to address fifteen minutes before. Involved all the murders I had committed around the East Village. Involved the instruction—who had it originated with?—that I had to strike him hard.

I was getting somewhere.

In fact, I am suddenly feeling just audacious enough to propose that if I had had a little more time that night in the rain with a sweet potato in my hand, I might actually have sliced through enough of my own mist to reach the conclusion that both Anthony and The Hat had been right, and that at the very least it would be better, much better, not to walk through Mr. Kindt's door. But about twenty feet after I had that realization, my promising train of thought was cut short by a punch in the mouth.

I don't know if you've ever been punched right in the middle of your face while you are walking fairly briskly through a dark, rain-spattered park with your head turned down and all your attention turned elsewhere. If you have, you will not be at all surprised to know that the blow came very close to knocking me out, and that I ended up on my back with my arms lying useless at my sides. I registered their immobility almost immediately, because my first instinct was to check my teeth to see if they were still there, and I couldn't. I moved my tongue, which I must have bitten, around inconclusively, then opened my mouth a little, then gave up.

They're still there, if that's what you're wondering, a voice said.

What? I said.

Your teeth—if that is what you're wondering, they're still there.

Of course they're still there, another voice said.

Why of course? I said.

Because I wasn't trying to knock them out, that's why. They would be out if I wanted them out.

Well, thanks for not wanting that, I said.

A face came into my field of vision then left it.

Another face did the same.

This isn't in the scenario, I said.

It's in the margins, written in lemon juice, one of the contortionists said.

Safety provision, the other said.

Where's Cornelius? I said.

Keep you from thinking too much.

Keep you from thinking too much in too much detail and fucking things up.

Cornelius wouldn't like that.

Neither would Mr. Kindt.

That's quite a pair.

Yeah, they go way back.

This last remark made them both laugh. Unpleasantly.

I put my head down on the pavement and shut my eyes.

You know, I said, in my quietest voice, I had you two all wrong. I thought you were the nice ones. I mean, I figured Cornelius was sketchy, maybe even sinister, and that the knockout wasn't nice, although she was nice, of course, I mean *obviously*, to look at, but that the two of you were the nicest. I guess I was wrong. I guess probably none of you are nice. Not even Tulip. Tulip, who found me. Who brought me in. Who does things for Mr. Kindt. Maybe they aren't nice things. Maybe she's got her own grudge. Maybe she's related to the Aris Kindt who died swimming. How old is she anyway? Maybe the Aris Kindt who died swimming was her father. Or maybe it's a grudge against me. Maybe she knew my dead aunt. Maybe my dead aunt was dear to her. I'll ask her about it later. She'll talk. No, she won't. I'll go ask The Hat. He seems to have answers. Who the fuck is he? Why exactly did Cornelius and Mr. Kindt decide to tell me about Lake Otsego? It's a closed system. No outside perspective. Nothing to confirm. No one to confirm it. Even The Hat—did Cornelius hire him? Did Mr. Kindt? To what end? What do I mean? But the two of you. Maybe you would be nice enough to explain this to me. I mean, my miscomprehension on such a basic point: you aren't nice. Do you think it's important? Tell me about yourselves. Where do you come from? Flesh yourselves out a little. What are your names? Who is everyone? What the fuck is going on?

Both faces were now back in my field of vision. They were very wet and very red and very, very close.

You hit him too hard, one of the faces said.

I did not hit him too hard, said the other.

o.k., fine, but he's unconscious.

I'm not unconscious, I said. I heard some kind of wet scraping sound. Someone smacked their lips.

You think he knows?

About tonight?

About poor old Lenny.

Nah, Cornelius and Kindt were careful.

Who is poor old Lenny? I said.

He's the accountant. Leonard Seligman, one of your victims.

My victims?

Let's just say he didn't make it.

Give him some smelling salts.

Who has smelling salts?

Shake him around a little.

Just let him lie there. There's plenty of time. The rain'll wake him up. He can dream about his great buddy, Mr. Kindt.

Laughter. Gales of it.

I am awake, I said. Their faces had vanished. All I could see was rain and dripping tree branches. After a while, though I wasn't sure if it could in fact be attributed to the rain, the use of my arms returned to me, as did that of various other tendons and muscles and limbs and nerve clusters, and I sat up.

Good, now I'm soaking fucking wet, I said.

It's time, Henry, Cornelius said, coming up behind me, putting his arms under my shoulders and helping me up.

As he helped me, I could see the contortionists, farther down the path, grinning unpleasantly. The knockout, too, had appeared, was sitting on a bench wearing a long black vinyl raincoat and holding a small gun.

Is that real? I asked Cornelius.

Of course not, none of this is real, Henry.

None of it?

He handed me a knife, a flat-handled silver buck knife.

What's this? I thought it was supposed to be a wire. I thought I was supposed to choke him until his throat bled.

Last-minute change.

What the fuck am I supposed to do with a knife?

You will make a line with it across Mr. Kindt's throat.

A line, I said.

A very straight line. Be sure to break the skin.

Cornelius smiled. I looked over my shoulder. The knockout was also smiling, as were the contortionists.

What was with the punch in the face?

It's time, Henry, Cornelius said. Mr. Kindt is waiting for you.

He was sitting cross-legged on his bed wearing black silk pajamas and a black silk sheet draped over his head.

What are you doing here so late, Henry? he said.

You know what I'm doing here, I said.

Mr. Kindt raised an eyebrow.

Fuck all this, I said.

What do you mean, dear boy?

I mean I'm tired of all this shit. You with your slop in bowls and heart monitors and beat-up books and being a crybaby because you killed someone a million years ago and took his name.

Mr. Kindt looked at me, a quizzical expression on his face.

I know about Lenny, I said.

Who is Lenny, Henry?

Your accountant.

I was eavesdropping in the rain. I heard about it. I know you took care of him. I know some fucking way or another I'm getting set up here to take a fall, and that the one doing the setting up is you.

He told me again that he didn't know what I was talking about so I yanked him out of bed and dragged him into the living room, sat him down on the floor beneath the window next to a purple orchid, and hit him with the ashtray. I went to the fridge and retrieved the bag of Mr. Kindt's blood, cut it open, and leaned over him with it and the serrated silver knife Cornelius had given me. Then I lifted the floorboard, retrieved the portfolio, and left him there. Lying in a heap in his black silk pajamas. Blue eyes open, rolled slightly back.

I very casually left the building and headed down Avenue B. Breathing hard but also whistling a little. Across and along Houston. Past Essex. Car lights shattering the rain. Impressed by the state Cornelius and Co. had managed to put me into. To Orchard. Along Orchard. The authenticity their little late-in-the-game revelation about setups and so forth must have leant my performance. My exquisite performance. The one I didn't yet know had been videotaped. Mr. Kindt's killer. Because of course he *was* killed. The authenticity was magnificent. Cut across the throat with the knife, the one I had brandished then left sitting on the floor by Mr. Kindt's head. I stopped. The little tattoo parlor was closed. Dark. No Tulip. Padlocked shut. I started thinking, and turned around.

Mr. Kindt lay beneath the window exactly as I had, I swear, left him, except that his throat was open. And there was no empty blood bag in the garbage under the sink. And no cheerful little note written by me as a flourish, saying that I would call tomorrow so that we could have lunch.

I leaned close to the window. I put my bloody hand on the cold, rain-splattered glass, pulled it away, and looked out at the park.

Then Tulip was there.

I didn't do this, I said. I mean, not *this*.

Save it, Henry, she said.

He's my friend, I said. My dear friend. I'm complicit. I know the story. I know Mr. Kindt isn't Mr. Kindt, or didn't used to be. I know he was trying to set me up, that he has set me up, hasn't he? Is that why he told me about Cooperstown—so that I'd have something else to think about? What's in this portfolio? Should I look?

I held up the small leather case and took a half step forward. I could see Mr. Kindt's hat and cape hanging by the door, his heart monitor dangling wires off the edges of the coffee table. I could see that Tulip, not smiling, was holding a gun.

I don't care what you did or didn't do, or know and don't know, you shouldn't have come back here, Henry, she said.

I could see her lift the gun and point it at me. I could see mist rising from Mr. Kindt, my dear dead friend dressed in black silk and lying with his throat open at my feet.

THIRTY

That's what I've most recently thought about it all, but probably now that I've discussed events with Mr. Kindt, who even much-diminished as he is likes a good talk, and who has been talking lately about how accuracy too often undoes us and precision too often blurs, I'm not so sure. The trouble is, despite the progress I'm supposed to be making, part of me isn't sure about anything these days. Things, as I've already let on, are a little confused, a little nebulous—to use one of the words that comes up when Mr. Kindt discusses the unavoidable tendency of past and present "to infect each other" here. They are growing more nebulous, not less. This increasing confusion stems in part, I suspect, from the fact that I have had to pay more and more frequent visits to Dr. Tulp's office. Not a great deal has changed about our meetings, except that the call button on her desk is no longer functioning and when she steps out into the hallway to yell for assistance no one comes.

Further complicating things is that several versions of what transpired during those last few hours were presented (by myself, by others) at my trial, some of which definitely have their appeal for me. In one, Mr. Kindt dies alone in his room. In another, he dies in company in his room. In one version of that version, I am there. It is just the two of us. It is dark. Mr. Kindt has called and I have come. He says there will be no need for any murdering, that it has been taken care of already, he can feel it coming on, so to speak. Mr. Kindt whispers something. One of the words he whispers is "false." Another is "wrong." Mr. Kindt dies happy, or at least smiling, unafraid in my arms.

Nevertheless, and Dr. Tulp, despite the adjustment in our relationship, has been quite firm on several occasions in getting me to admit this, it is the version I describe above—or anyway, the prosecutor's version of that version, which was, as I said, captured at its climactic moment on videotape by a camera hidden in Mr. Kindt's closet, one that is supposed to have been turned on by Mr. Kindt (he says he can't remember doing so and that, because he was unconscious, he has no idea, "only a very strong suspicion, Henry, since after all I am *here* with *you*," about who actually finished him off), which is described and discussed and made a mockery of during the trial—that burns the most brightly for me. It is in this version that I am sentenced in a courtroom resembling the murky interior of a water tower by a judge I could never quite see and sent here, or someplace very much like here, it is not heaven and I'm not leaving, so you can perhaps understand why such details now mean considerably less to me than, say, my next little talk with Dr. Tulp or next visit from my dear old aunt or next awful, windswept dream.

It means little to me that, in this version, a prosecutor describes Mr. Kindt's last moments as horrific, the vanished Tulip as blameless, and myself as a guileless, lovesick fool (in this context, they point out that I have had a yellow tulip tattooed over my heart). "We have here an individual so depraved that even in the face of overwhelming evidence, he continues to maintain his story that the murdered man, who the perpetrator has told us took him in and showed him great kindness, paid to be subjected to this deadly procedure, and that mysterious colleagues took part in helping the victim set him up. An individual, I add in conclusion, who has put forward an outlandish and irrelevant story about identity theft and an improbable, unverifiable murder that occurred half a century ago in upstate New York in order to muddy the waters and falsely cast suspicion upon others."

I maintain my innocence in the face of what is again referred to as overwhelming evidence that the so-called murders arranged by Cornelius and the contortionists and the knockout were arranged by me and by me alone. Which is to say that everyone the police talked to, whom I told them to talk to, deny, in this version, having ever dealt with anyone but me. The fact that the alleged crime was committed in the context of so much trauma and suffering throughout the great city of New York, by a known stalker and incompetent hustler, one who "cooked up" a "fortunately short-lived, morally repugnant" service, which served as a cover for acts of significant robbery, and at least one additional act of real murder—of an accountant, documents belonging to whom were found, along with documents belonging to Mr. Kindt, in a portfolio on my person—is also, with a shocking lack of eloquence, touched upon by the prosecutor in this version, and also means little to me.

That I say these things mean little to me is not meant to imply that I consider my comportment, in this version, as being in any way defensible. It is just that I am aware—and my own much-diminished Mr. Kindt, now that we have begun discussing it all, has confirmed the likelihood of this for me—that this is only one version among several, and that no matter how many people believe it, it does not command primacy.

In another version, you see, Mr. Kindt dies with a smile on his lips, holding each of our hands, grateful that his "tedious suffering," as he puts it, has been abridged. And in another, just as valid, Mr. Kindt doesn't die at all, he continues living, we all continue living, though I don't say we're happy about it.

ACKNOWLEDGMENTS

While many books informed and inspired this one, W. G. Sebald's *The Rings of Saturn,* translated from the German by Michael Hulse, provided key thematic and linguistic irritants throughout the writing of *The Exquisite,* e.g., falsification, death, long-standing vectors of destruction, herring, silk, the historical perspective, elective affinities, and, by no means least, Aris Kindt himself, the half-hidden centerpiece of Rembrandt's *The Anatomy Lesson.* Realizing when the project began to take shape that I was far from alone in my enthusiasm for Sebald's narratives and in my desire to manifest that enthusiasm in a work of my own, I decided not to try, as it seemed to me so many were trying, to "do a Sebald," i.e., truffle pages with visual images, eschew novelistic sleight of hand in favor of quietly patterned and heavily mediated observation, and inject the whole with a steady drip of melancholia. Ezra Pound called the results of this sort of homage dilution and I was not interested in diluting. The approach then was to write a book unlike one Sebald would have written, while taking up and recasting his favorite themes and obsessions. An improbable ghost noir set in New York's East Village involving portentous nightmares, a mock-murder service, and great quantities of pickled herring seemed to fit the bill.

I should also mention: Sir Thomas Browne's *Hydriotaphia,* that great treatise on modes of burial, which is not coincidentally discussed in *The Rings of Saturn,* is channeled at length by Cornelius the night our hero first meets him, and briefly by Tulip on the platform of Grand Central

Station. The imaginary texts, etc. on page 137 are taken from Browne's *Musaeum Clausum*. Bits and lovely pieces of Ben Katchor's marvelous *Cheap Novelties: The Pleasures of Urban Decay, with Julius Knipl, Real Estate Photographer* (moon lamps, aluminum paperweights, water stations, Roman Street, Optaline eye salve, etc.), bubble up here and there throughout the pages of *The Exquisite,* helping, it is hoped, to make no bones about the partially dreamt quality of Henry's New York (not to mention his experiences therein). All of our New Yorks, after all, are partially dreamt. Many, like Henry's, are shaped by the brilliant dreamers who have been there before us.

The image on page 131 is a detail from
Hans Holbein the Younger's *The Dance of Death.*

COLOPHON

The Exquisite was designed at Coffee House Press,
in the historic warehouse district
of downtown Minneapolis.
Fonts include Village and Copperplate Gothic.

FUNDER ACKNOWLEDGMENTS

Coffee House Press is an independent nonprofit literary publisher. Our books are made possible through the generous support of grants and gifts from many foundations, corporate giving programs, individuals, and through state and federal support. Coffee House Press receives general operating support from the Minnesota State Arts Board, through an appropriation by the Minnesota State Legislature and from the National Endowment for the Arts, a federal agency. Coffee House receives major funding from the McKnight Foundation, and from Target. Coffee House also receives significant support from: an anonymous donor; the Elmer and Eleanor Andersen Foundation; the Buuck Family Foundation; the Bush Foundation; the Patrick and Aimee Butler Family Foundation; the Foundation for Contemporary Arts; Gary Fink; Stephen and Isabel Keating; Seymour Kornblum and Gerri Lauter; the Lenfesty Family Foundation; Rebecca Rand; the law firm of Schwegman, Lundberg, Woessner & Kluth, P.A.; Charles Steffey and Suzannah Martin; the James R. Thorpe Foundation; the Archie D. and Bertha H. Walker Foundation; Thompson West; the Woessner Freeman Family Foundation; the Wood-Hill Foundation; and many other generous individual donors.

This activity is made possible
in part by a grant from the
Minnesota State Arts Board,
through an appropriation by the
Minnesota State Legislature
and a grant from the National
Endowment for the Arts.

MINNESOTA
STATE ARTS BOARD

TARGET.

To you and our many readers across the country,
we send our thanks for your continuing support.

Good books are brewing at coffeehousepress.org